THE RISE & FALL OF THE SCANDAMERICAN DOMESTIC

# THE RISE & FALL
# OF THE
# SCANDAMERICAN DOMESTIC

STORIES

CHRISTOPHER MERKNER

COFFEE HOUSE PRESS
MINNEAPOLIS
2014

Coffee House Press books are available to the trade through our primary distributor, Consortium Book Sales & Distribution, cbsd.com or (800) 283-3572. For personal orders, catalogs, or other information, write to: info@coffeehousepress.org.

Coffee House Press is a nonprofit literary publishing house. Support from private foundations, corporate giving programs, government programs, and generous individuals helps make the publication of our books possible. We gratefully acknowledge their support in detail in the back of this book.

Visit us at coffeehousepress.org.

LIBRARY OF CONGRESS CIP INFORMATION

Merkner, Christopher.
[Short stories. Selections]
The rise & fall of the Scandamerican domestic : stories / by Christopher Merkner.—First edition.
pages cm
ISBN 978-1-56689-338-1 (PBK.)
ISBN 978-1-56689-344-2 (E-BOOK)
1. Scandinavian Americans—Fiction. 2. Domestic fiction, American.
I. Title. II. Title: Rise and fall of the Scandamerican domestic : stories.
PS3613.E7567R57 2014
813'.6—DC23
2013003664

PRINTED IN THE UNITED STATES
FIRST EDITION | FIRST PRINTING

FOR MOLLY

# CONTENTS

If Swedish intercourse is problematic and the
"model society" surprisingly unsociable,
the Swede is perhaps unique in often being able to
feel more at his ease among foreigners than among
his own kith and kin.

—**PAUL BRITTEN AUSTIN,** *on being Swedish*


The Swedes in America cannot be considered a
people; they could only be material . . .

—**ARTHUR LANDFORS, "POET IN SWEDISH AMERICA"**

# OF PIGS AND CHILDREN

Life seduces from afar. This is a French concept
I believe, though I have never been to France and
can speak no French and have never been exposed
to any French literature that might corroborate this
sensation I have about things in the world becoming more attractive, more alluring, the further away
one gets from them—

And really, with every story my mother forces on
me about her pig, I am happily finding myself slip-
ping further and further away from her kitchen
table. I have no interest in what she has to say about
this pig; I am thinking instead of my dead uncle. I
am thinking about having accidentally gaffed him in
the temple with one of my musky bucktails on a
very simple and heaving backcast, and the problem
here, as I see it, is this: I am feeling an unexpected

excitement in not telling my mother about her brother's death. It is exciting me to withhold this information. The longer I wait, the longer I sit here listening to her speak, the further away I get from her and the trauma I have undergone, the more satisfied I feel.

It's curious.

I could easily tell her, of course. The death was not my fault. I am not guilty of any heinous crime. I have not fulfilled some secret vendetta against my uncle. I can come away clean.

But at some point, if I continue to say nothing about having killed her brother, she will want to know how the man disappeared. She will call the police; there will be a manhunt; I will be questioned, as I am the last known person to have been seen with him, and less than twenty-four hours ago; I will confess everything I know to the police; I will *appear* guilty of a heinous crime; and I will be hung, or shot, or put away in a cage forever. And let me make this emphatically clear: this appeals to me, very much. I like this possibility. I find pleasure in *not* telling her about her brother's death because part of me—a pressing and primal and mysterious part of me—is curiously drawn to the prospect of being guilty of something for which I am technically not guilty.

But still—

This pig of hers, of which she has been talking for the past half hour, is in my lap. I am petting it. It is a Vietnamese potbelly, which were apparently very popular about seven or eight years ago in the upscale suburban circles of Madison and Chicago, but have since fallen by the wayside, for people like my mother to pick up at rural flea markets at next to no cost.

This is the type of drivel my mother is trying to meaningfully convey to me as I begin removing myself from her severe and penetrating face. She has not asked why I have arrived at her house so early on a Sunday morning. She has asked me nothing of myself. But she pauses in her steady, tight-lipped monologue and expects me to respond to her.

"Well, that is an interesting thought," I say to her, though to be sure, I only have the most general sense of what she has been saying.

"You know," she replies, "it *is* an interesting thing to say, because the wildest thing about it is that I'm pretty sure she understands me the same way I understand her. We understand each other, you see."

"You understand each other," I repeat. She is in her thick gray bathrobe, the one she has worn all my life, pulled tightly to her neck.

"I think it's as plain as day, really," my mother confides. "Anyone with eyes and who is honest with themselves will see that she is *the* most demonstrative pig they have ever laid eyes on." I don't know what my mother means exactly by *demonstrative,* but I'd be willing to bet that if she means that this pig shows a lot of expression in its face, or that the pig wears, as the saying goes, its heart out on its sleeve, well then I guess I might rightly call my uncle Ackvund, at the moment when he understood he had a twelve-inch musky lure sticking through his eye socket, *demonstrative.*

*Helpless,* though, seems to be the more fitting adjective. In fact, I don't honestly know what *helpless* is, if it isn't the image of poor Ackvund swatting aimlessly at his entire face, patting his cheeks and forehead like a blind man searching the ground for pocket change until (and I'd be lying if I said that I hadn't seen this coming) he hooked one of his fingers on the same hook that was projecting out of his eye. The barb, then, if you can picture this, went right through the fingernail—

A *shish kabob* is what some of you city people with no conscience might call it. But I think *helpless* is really the word I want here.

"Well, that's another interesting point," I say to my mother, when she hesitates between sentences again.

She squints at me.

"It is," I assure her.

"What did I just say to you?"

"About the pig," I say. "About Lala. That was a really good point you made."

"Well it *is* a good point, because I just don't think enough people realize that these animals, and most animals for that matter, have a remarkable sense of hearing. They hear marvelously. And they *listen*—oh, they listen. I've seen this one turn her head to me and seriously think about, or at least *look* like she's seriously thinking about—"

My mother laughs at this point and looks affectionately at the warm beast in my lap. She becomes earnest again and continues. "She *seriously* thinks about what it is I've just told her." I am petting this pig as my mother begins another story. Her hard head (the pig's hard head) has some hairs on it that feel like metal wires and other hairs that are really quite soft. The pig's eyes are closed and it is snoring.

I am attracted to this animal in a strange and strong way. Its warm body, I think, is what appeals to me most right now. It is making my thighs sweaty. Its eyes are closed. Its head is propped against my hip with arrogance and nonchalance. It is breathing slowly.

It is snoring. It is encouraging me to relax.

And it is important that I relax, I think, because I have not done so since the moment I first stood up in the boat and looked at my uncle, and he, blood flowing down his cheek, looked helplessly back at me. Recalling this moment even now, I have to say, undoes much of what this pig has been doing for me by way of relaxation—

Oh I tried to help him, of course. *I* wasn't the helpless, demonstrative one. I didn't balk. I didn't blanch. Not at first. I wasn't by any means *paralyzed*. In fact, I moved toward him immediately and

tried to calm his violent and, as I said, aimless patting of his own face. But I couldn't stop him until it
was too late, until he had stuck his finger all the way
through the hook, past the barb. When I finally did
get my hands on him, I attempted to comfort him
by rubbing his shoulders, as if he had caught a chill.
This was instinctive, and for many obvious reasons
it not only did *not* calm him down, it actually
prompted a litany of anguished wails, the most
coherent of which was, "Get it out. It itches. Like
Jesus Christ. Get it out."

"Well," I say to my mother, when she has
stopped talking again, "I don't know."

"What don't you know?"

"I don't know what to say about that," I say. I
look at the gray kitchen in which I was raised. Not
a basket has once been removed from the wall, not
a framed picture altered or updated. Dust covers
everything.

"Say about what?"

"About what you just said," I say. "About Missy.
About the pig."

"I didn't say anything just now about the pig. I
was telling you about my back."

"Do you have any orange juice?"

She gets up. *Now,* I realize, would be the time to tell her about the gaffing. We have, at long last, ended the conversation about the pig. Now would be the time, I think, if ever there was a time, to tell my mother that her brother is dead, and that I have killed him unwittingly, and that *this* is the reason I have come over to her house on Sunday morning and am sitting in her kitchen chair.

She pours me a glass of orange juice and sits down. She is looking at me.

"You're not a good listener," she says.

"I'm not," I say. "This is most certainly true."

"Your father wasn't a good listener either," she says. Her lips are chapped. Her charcoal hair is pulled back tightly off her chalk-white forehead in something like a ponytail.

I say nothing. I have nothing to add to this. I don't think it wise to discuss my father, whom she has long hated, at this juncture in the conversation. From my perspective, anyway, we've got enough trouble brewing. And she must sense this too, that she has made a mistake in comparing her dead and unloved husband's name to my own, because she drops this line of conversation and points to the pig in my lap.

"This one, you know, keeps me up till all hours of the night."

I smile. "I believe that."

"My little restless lover," she laughs, not smiling.

I look down at the pig, because my mother is looking down at the pig when she says this. Its nose is wet. I think I could play with the liquid draining from its nose for a long, long time. I am not gross, I think, for admitting this. The liquid is glistening and fascinating to touch, and that the pig is letting me play with its slimy nose—letting me, in fact, stick my second and fourth fingers nearly all the way up into its nostrils, rotate my fingers in gentle supplications, slip my fingers out, and pull the slickness away from the rim of its gaping and bumpy apertures—only makes it more captivating.

This is a fascination, as I have said, that helps me realize again how universally seductive life is at a distance. Pulling at the pig's nostrils gives me the sense of doing things from a long way away. It is as if I am not, myself, even doing it. I feel as though this pig would have to be conscious of me doing what I am doing for me to be doing it at all. And this may be what the French call (and really it is just shameful that I say this at all after already admitting my complete ignorance of the French language) the motive or the instinct or the nature of the *voyeur*—

And how I wish I was but a voyeur at that pivotal moment when I, at length, forced myself to sit down, swallow my disbelief, grab the oars, and row my uncle and myself back to shore after the gaffing. I would give or do anything to have been then where I am right now.

And so too would have my uncle, I suspect, because when it came to rowing the boat, Ackvund knew better than anyone else (I can still hear him scoffing) that I had a lead left arm. Since childhood I have had a hell of a time keeping the boat true to its course, and, as a result, Ackvund had always taken it on himself to row us in and out of the vast chop we used to call Big Lake.

There is little doubt in my mind therefore why, when I sat down to take the oars, my uncle began weeping for the first time. To this point, he had been nothing short of Norwegian royalty: not a word spoken, not a tear shed. But then I could see quite plainly that besides the crying (you really couldn't mistake it) he had just wet his pants. He was crumbling right there before me. Surely he must have thought that my taking over the oars would be the anguished end of us both—

But I will say this in my defense: I rowed hard, as hard as I could and as fast as I could, and followed as best I could the instructions I had heard all my life about rowing a boat—that is, pick a spot on the far shore (tree, cabin) and keep your eyes fastened to that landmark the entire time, so that you are always pulling away from the same place and heading, in theory, to the place directly its opposite, which, for only the most romantic northerner, would be the intended terminus.

God help me, my landmark kept switching from one tree to the next, one cabin to another (no fault of my own, really, given the dire circumstances and the uncanny likenesses of all the trees and cabins in this part of the country). What I was losing in accuracy, I was gaining in unprecedented speed—

Indeed, we might have been clipping along at more than ten miles per hour when I suddenly realized we were not headed toward our own dock, but the Halvorsteds' dock perhaps a quarter mile off the mark.

To change directions at this point seemed to me a tremendous impossibility. I looked to our dock (and mind, here, that I was craning my neck a full 180 degrees, and at times more, as my body was facing toward the opposite side of the lake, my back to the approaching shoreline and Halvorsteds' dock), and in that very brief moment in which I had turned to calculate the distance from our dock to the Halvorsteds', having established, as I say, so much water speed, we struck the oncoming dock squarely and to my complete surprise. I pitched backwards, but clung to the oars. My uncle, however, had no sense at all of what was approaching—

I heard him shout once, and it was as robust and tortured a howl as I had ever heard in my life from another human. I spun around quickly and the only trace of him I could see were his legs pointing straight up in the air, as in rigor mortis, and my bowing rod, jammed between the inner gunwale and my own seat, its line taught and crystalline and vibrating and still anchored horribly in my uncle's head—

"Just stop doing that!" my mother says to me.

"Doing what?" I slip my finger out of the pig's nostril.

"Thank you," she says. Her jaw is clenched. "Christ."

"What?" I say. "She likes it."

"No, she does not."

"She isn't *moving*."

As though it has been cued, the damn pig moves. It stirs in its sleep and looks up at me. It snorts. It rises shakily, because it is standing on my lap, and my thighs are proving to be a less-than-stable platform for its cloven, bowed legs. It wobbles and snorts. This pig is sexy, I'm not going to pretend any longer it isn't so. I'm not going to act as though its stunted proportions and its angled, little mouth do not stir in me some perverse kinship.

I grab its chubby sides and wiggle its fat. It isn't kinky, it isn't grotesque, it's just funny and vaguely erotic.

"Stop it!" my mother shouts. She gets up from her chair and leans over me, to take the pig away.

"All right, all right," I say. Gently, I push her arms away from the pig.

"What is wrong with you?" she asks. "Why are you here? What are you doing here?"

I pause. I take in the odor of this old room.

"I killed your brother," I say.

She makes a face.

"He's down in the cabin," I say. "Dead."

She says nothing. She thinks I'm kidding. I shake my head.

"He is," I say. "I killed him. It's my fault. Go look."

"Get out of my house," she says.

"Mother," I say.

"Get out," she says again.

I don't go anywhere. Where am I going to go? I have this pig on my lap and we need to call the police. I cannot run away. Running will get me nowhere except further from this situation, and frankly, I'm as far *and* as close to this problem as I want to get. I am in the throes of voyeur fulfillment. I am not in trouble; I am posturing as trouble. I am hovering over conflict like smoke above fire. I am the contour of wrongdoing, the specter of guilt—

And for what it's worth, I tried to call the police from the cabin, when I first got Ackvund back to his home, but by then it was too late; he was dead. And anyway the phone was dead too, because Ackvund never paid his phone bills, which was, of course, the main reason I was out fishing with him—to give the old guy, who had been losing some of his marbles, a little company and guidance, perhaps remind him very gently to pay his bills and take his medication.

It occurred to me at one point (and I can't remember if it was on the dock or up by the cabin or just after I had broken through the Halvorsteds' cabin window after I discovered no one was home) to stop and give Ackvund a more thorough looking over. I studied his face very closely. His cheeks were covered with blood, and both of his eyes were closed, sealed shut with a sheet of golden crust. He was scowling. He wasn't talking though. As I've alluded to, we are not a family of French origin; we are Norwegians, and this silence in the face of sustained anguish was not extraordinary behavior for my uncle or anyone else I know.

In any case, he must have felt me breathing on his face as I looked at him, because he opened his one eye, the one that of course did not have the hook stuck in it and the hand covering it, and when he opened his eye, I decided the best course of action would be to explain the nature of our predicament to him. I looked him square in that eye and I said very sternly and very clearly, as though he was hard of hearing, "Ackvund, you have a fishing hook stuck in your eye. Don't worry. We are going to get it out of there." I formed a hook with one of my fingers and demonstrated for him on my head how and where the hook had penetrated his skull, and how it had come out of his eye and through his finger.

This was a mindless effort, I realize now. He only looked at me briefly, then closed his eye again. The color of his face faded. I caught him by the elbow just as he began to slouch and the pain in this—as I had grabbed the elbow of his hooked arm—brought him instantly back among the living.

This pig is remarkably black. It is vividly black. Shimmering black. It is sleeping again, sleeping so soundly in fact that its feet quiver. Its ears are soft on the inside, coarse on the outside. I've mentioned this before, I realize, but it's worth repeating. I do not have hair so distinct. Why, then, should this beast? And does it matter? No, it does not. What matters more is my increasing desire for this animal.

I put it down on the floor. It is beginning to arouse me—

I want my mother to return home so that we might continue our earlier conversation. I am finding that in this silence, my recollections of yesterday morning with my uncle are becoming horribly acute. They are lulling me into a sadness I cannot see myself overcoming.

My mother, I have neglected to say, has left her own house and driven, I suspect, though she did not say this to me, to her brother's cabin, where she will find his dead body supine on the couch with the television on. She has not yet returned. I imagine she is experiencing something a lot like what I am right now—a sense of peering into somebody else's bedroom, the door left slightly ajar—

This is odd. But I have to wonder if something as odd as this was crossing my uncle Ackvund's mind after I broke into the Halvorsteds' cabin and found no telephone. His face, when I informed him that I had found no phone, glossed over; a grin flashed, and then his skull appeared to sink. And it pains me to remember what I did then, seeing his face. Truly, I had no idea I could do what I then decided to do—that is, hoist my uncle up, from under his knees, and carry him on my shoulder out to the front of the Halvorsteds' cabin, and all the way to the road.

My uncle, you should know, could not have weighed less than 250 pounds at the time, and I had no choice but to put him down several times, leaning him against the side of the cabin while I caught my breath. After nearly one half hour of defying gravity, I was only able to get him as far as the front of the driveway, near the Halvorsteds' garage. Exhausted, I decided I could carry him no farther, was in fact doing him a grave disservice by trying, and I ran instead to the front of the cabin to look for something, *anything*, that might aid in my rescue.

Mercifully, I found a wheelbarrow and pushed it to him, laid him in it, then wheeled him as quickly as I could out to the road—then there was the waiting, much like I find myself waiting right now—

Its belly, this pig's belly, is so tender that when I roll it over on its back and press my hand against its stomach, the impression of my hand is outlined quite clearly in its fat, white flesh. It squirms as if I've pressed too hard, but it is a good-natured pig, and scrambles to its feet and comes to me again, snorting.

Its sounds are not at all unlike the whimpering noises my uncle was making as he waited beside me in the wheelbarrow. I found myself ignoring, to the extent that I could, my uncle's wailing while we were waiting at the side of the road for someone to drive past. But County Road H is not a busy thoroughfare, and after ten minutes or so of his anguished weeping, I went to him and put my hands on his shoulders and looked him square in the eye. I spoke to him, and this (that's right, I'm sure of it now) was when I talked to Ackvund as though he were deaf and explained to him the precise nature of all his trouble; this was when I made the little fishing hook with my finger and demonstrated for him, by sticking my finger-hook near my eye, the way in which the hook had come through his temple and out his socket. And this was when, at last, I took the rod from his fierce clutches and clipped the line with my teeth, leaving the lure to dangle and sway freely— freely at last—from his face.

I remember that he was, in a word, *helpless* after I did this, and that I was starting to lose him. I had begun wheeling him back toward *his* cabin (which I knew was no short distance from the Halvorsteds') when I saw one of the Eckers rumbling toward us in his red combine. I flagged the machine down, and the man inside—Jimmy, I think—offered to let us jump on the back. Foolishly, I took the offer.

For twenty minutes (and I dare say they were the worst twenty minutes of Ackvund's long and loving life) we vibrated, rattled, shook, bumped, and rocked all along the graveled edge of the road—and this was *after* the procedure of getting Ackvund settled onto the back of the machine. Eckers, I might mention, never once stepped out of the air-conditioned cab of his vehicle to offer assistance, leaving it to me to pull the wounded soul up onto the hood of the threshing board by myself.

In any case, it didn't take me all of those twenty minutes to realize I had made a tragic mistake in not continuing with the wheelbarrow—besides what must have been torturous and incessant vibration for my uncle, Eckers refused to drive faster than several miles per hour, with the result that we were going absolutely nowhere in a bloody, blistering hurry. From my uncle's eye, that twelve-inch bucktail (I can still see it) swayed back and forth like a metronome, ticking—

"Please put her down," my mother says. She has come through the back door.

"I'd rather not," I say. I hold the pig away from her. I stand up. "Why do you look like that? You're scaring me, Mom."

"*I'm* scaring *you*?" she says. "What did you do to him, you monster? Why is he so filthy? Where did you two go?"

There's a look in her eye when she says this that betrays her seduction. Her face has never been so radiant. She is feverish. She demands that I give her the pig. She slaps my back with her open hand. She wants the pig, she wants her brother, she wants answers. She wants in a way she has never before wanted. If only her violent hitting of my back could speak.

"Stop it, Mother," I say. "Leave the pig alone. Let me just hold it."

"The police are coming!" she shouts.

"Yes," I say. "Sure. They should be."

I am holding the pig away from me, my arms extended, my hands under its warm, hairy armpits, my back screening my mother from taking it away.

The pig is looking over its shoulder, as though it is trying to figure out what I want to do with it. I bring its face to mine, to give it a kiss on the forehead before I put it down on the floor, and it slips its quick little tongue into my mouth like a dart. The tongue flickers into and out of my mouth several times, though my lips are tightly pursed. It's a very narrow tongue and it is very warm. I open my mouth wide and let it in.

My mother gasps.

She takes a cookie sheet out of the drying rack and slams it across my back. Though the pan is flimsy, the edge of the stupid thing catches my elbow—my funny bone—and I drop the pig. It sprawls on the floor and squeals. It looks up at me, confused, and scrambles away.

I lunge after it.

"Get away from her!" my mother shouts. There is a knock at the door. I look up at my mother and my mother looks at the door. She looks the way Ackvund did when I dumped him off the side of the combine into the ditch and ran like hell to get my car; that is, she looks fundamentally torn, split between two sides of a decision.

Don't let me deceive you by way of breeziness here: Ackvund was most likely dead by the time I dumped him off the side of the combine and ran. He had rolled into the slop in the culvert, and when I'd returned with my car, flipped him over onto his back, taken his pulse, and felt for his breath, there was no doubt he was absolutely dead and I couldn't think of bringing him into the hospital as he was, so I drove him back to his cabin only to find his phone was, as I've already said, not working.

The police officer knocks again. My mother goes to the door. I run into the dining room and look under the table for the pig. I want this pig more than I want anything else in the world. I can't explain this. It's under a chair. I go after it, swipe and miss. I chase it through the living room and into the bedroom. I lunge for this precious squalling creature before it can get underneath the bed, and I pull it out by its haunches. It squeals. It struggles. I pull it close. The cop yells at me, but I don't stop. I bring the beast to my face, and I kiss it, and it licks me back, and when it licks my open mouth its narrow tongue is like a fire-hot poker in my throat. The police officer yells, my mother yells, and I am mouth to mouth with this pig, and I am sucking, siphoning its lungs for air, and its little tongue is searing hot and sour against my gums, and I am seeing myself do this with eyes that are not entirely my own—

They are my mother's eyes, this police officer's, and they are the eyes of a nephew watching the hands of some stranger doing this, holding and kissing a pig, and this is not my mother's pig falling to the ground, and this is not a pig scampering under a bed, and these are not my hands being forced and cuffed behind my back, and these are not my rights being read to me off a list of rights I know nothing about, and this is not my mother weeping and reaching under the bed for her pig while her son is taken away by the police officer, and these are not her hands holding her pig in front of me, taunting me on the front lawn, torturing me in front of the gaping neighbors of my past life as I am led away like some pilloried criminal from another time. As far as I can see, these are the hands of absence and desire and hunting, and these are the hands that all of my life I have been using as my own.

## CHECK THE BABY

The grandest joke about the baby is who goes up to check on him. Because whoever goes up always wakes him, and no one wants him woken, not at three weeks, not ever.

We've started promising sexual favors to the one who goes up—the one who wakes him and therein coddles, swaddles, bottles—you see, your entire life sucked as by some insect, pest.

The stakes are not low, I might add. I have 4,027 blowjobs coming my way someday, it's not exactly clear when; and my wife has roughly fourteen hours of French-style kissing.

These favors might accumulate without realization until the cows come home. And I hate to say it, but at a certain point the stakes climb so that the thing being wagered against tumbles into the ridiculous and you have no idea what you're really facing or avoiding. At which point, I am confronted about my drinking.

When my wife cleans house, she's surgical: "I think you're drinking because if you're drunk you know I can't trust you to go upstairs and check on him."

"That's flattering," I say.

"I also think you're no longer interested in the sex we've been bartering."

"Is it really a form of fair trade, what we're doing there with that?"

The grandest joke about the baby isn't the sort of joke one laughs at. But when I'm offered sex at the grocery store by a strange woman, the entire child-rearing phase of my life looks rather like a farce.

"I have a child," I tell her, and she says she knows this, has solicited me for this very reason. "But you would never see the child," I tell her. "Under no circumstances."

But she just wants the smell of them. Can't actually *stand* children, but she loves their smell, wants to eat the smell.

"You're a fine lady."

But we live in one of these new communities that orbits a single, fantastic, oversized grocery store, and I keep passing her in the aisles—Shoes and Pets and Car Gear. I smile to be kind, and she keeps saying things like, "Hey, offer's still on the table." Or, one time she boldly whiffs the air and says, "Three . . . no, four weeks. Right?"

I shudder, but I'm a little drunk on four vanilla bottles from Baking, so at some point I titter—

Yes, I commit adultery against my god, my wife and son, and every time the blowjobs and French-style kissing are mentioned I'm nearly vomiting, and I don't mind saying my journeys upstairs to my silent-asleep son, just to make sure he hasn't inexplicably stopped breathing, hurt.

# IN LAPLAND

On Thursday my wife returns from work and says she needs some color in the house, can't live in this cell-hole another minute, what have we done to bring ourselves to this way of living at our age, we aren't twenty-five-year-old twits, not anymore. Country Rill is the green she shows me in a magazine. "Look at that," she says, thrusting the glossy in my face, "and tell me it wouldn't change everything." I cannot tell her this. It's time to do something, truly. We are in agreement. It is time. We have waited a long time, and at our age we can no longer afford to wait to do anything. Everything must be done last month, when there was time.

On Saturday we compare Country Rill prices at four stores—none of the Country Rills green the way Country Rill greened in the magazine. A woman at one of these places is juggling the questions of five other customer couples, each team looking plaintive and positioning themselves for sustained explanation of paint application.

The woman fielding these questions has no time for this. She is a rough sort of woman, a person made hard by excessive painting, I think, and not the person to articulate the ways of reducing such hardness. She is saying to another couple, "Look, paint isn't permanent. It can always be fixed. You just go and you just do it and you can do it again."

When she turns a few minutes of her time to us, she studies her store's litmus-looking paint sample against my wife's picture in the magazine. "Same thing," she concludes.

"No," my wife says. "Not at all the same."

The woman brings the paint litmus and the magazine up closer to her face, lifts her glasses off her nose, props them on her forehead, and seems almost to smell the Country Rill. She is very serious. "No," she finally says, "not the same. But they're as close as can be."

"You have thousands of paints," my wife says. "Can't you mix a blend to get it to look like this?"

The woman looks up, hands the magazine back to us, and studies my wife's face. "Yeah," she says, "but it still won't be what you want."

There is silence. My wife is looking at me. She wants me to confront this woman. I think about what to say to coerce her to make the color. Then the woman speaks again. "Look, if I mix this paint for you, to try to get you this color, you won't like it. Trust me. You have to just get a color and like it. This"—she points to the magazine in my wife's hands—"this isn't your paint. It's someone else's, and you cannot have it. That's the way it is with paint."

This enrages my wife, who contends that she has never heard anything more ridiculous in her life. "Color is a science, not an art. Paint is not unique. Color can be manufactured to a precise and desired specific quality. We aren't dealing in the subjective," she says, and I agree. But because we're both originally from the Madison, Wisconsin, area, we've reserved all this direct outrage for the car ride home and really let the car windows have it.

*

All day Sunday we're on broadband scrolling over online paint resources. By sunset we have selected a Country Rill from a company in Pennsylvania and had it shipped overnight to the house. We pay an ungodly figure to overnight this paint, but there is no looking back: when it comes to paint, when it comes to everything at this point in our lives, cost is negligible. We charge it. We have no time for savings. All the saving we've been doing, all that's over. For the first time that weekend, we eat dinner without rushing. We have even turned on the television. It's the last supper.

*

We lie awake and talk about timing. How long does it take to paint trim? Can you paint in the evening, or should you paint in daylight? Does daylight diminish the quality of the paint, does direct sunlight undermine the integrity of the pigments? Should we paint every night of the week, or wait and complete the paint job all in one weekend?

I say, "I don't think I could do that, physically."

My wife reaches across my nude chest and seizes the telephone to call her sister. I can hear her sister's answers to the questions.

"You're freaking out. You're freaking out about nothing. Do whatever you want. Paint a little, paint a lot. People with a lot less education than you—people in Lapland—paint all the time and have no problem with it. Don't make it a problem. Paint when it feels natural to paint. There's no right way to paint. When our house got painted, we didn't even want it painted. It just happened. We were like, 'Well, I guess we'll have a painted house now.'"

Her condescension is a wet metal rod—a horse bit—in my mouth.

When they've finished and phone is back in cradle, I remind my wife that her sister has a cardiologist husband to pay for a professional job on their house, that it was a luxurious position to say it didn't matter what you did with paint, luxurious to believe you could do whatever the hell you wanted with the trim and all things would come out right in the end. Of course things will not come out right if you do not do them deliberately and thoughtfully.

My wife doesn't want to hear it. She flips a hand at me.

"And," I say, "to the matter of education and the poor subjects in Lapland: your sister has no idea how many people are actually painting in Lapland, very likely none."

\*

I dream of kneeling and working by the fireplace, those shit corners. What size brush should I use? And the tape job. That blue stickless tape. Of the trim along the floor, the carpeting.

\*

By Monday colleagues ask me my story, say things like, "What's your deal?" and I tell them.

"Oh my god!" one of them says, a woman I dated years ago and who seems determined to maintain an ongoing interest in my personal life. "You are going to do such a good job! I can completely see that for you, for your house! Your wife must just be like, 'Ah!'"

The males don't have a response at all to the painting question, only that I've shared anything about my domestic life with this old girlfriend. Do I think she won't somehow take advantage of this personal information, ask, for example, to come over and see it—help even, somehow? They laugh.

They haven't married yet, these guys. They have no idea what lies ahead. I try to level with them: "Can you paint trim every night or does this make the job uneven? Can paint go bad or change color if it's left too long?"

They look at me and shrug. One of them answers, "Keep that shit to yourself. Trust me, you don't want people telling you what's best for you and your wife."

"I'm talking objectively," I protest. "What's best for paint, generally speaking?"

"That's like asking what's best for cement, generally. It all depends on what kind of cement you want. Rough, textured, flat, matte, shiny. I can't tell you what you want. Anyway, even when you know what you want, to a certain degree you're just going to have to take what you get. You can't control cement. That's the bitch of Mother Nature."

\*

That evening, the sun is at an odd angle, gleaming off the cans on our front stoop. They have arrived. I yank them each inside the house and read their instructions over and over. It's exhausting. I feel woozy, the smell of the cans and of the future with the cans. I'm predicting the cans' smell. I close my eyes . . .

I open them, and my wife's ready. She throws her bags on the floor and tears off her shirt and slacks. She's in her underwear before I've sat upright. "Let's go," she says. "Get that lid off. Did you shake it? Stir it."

I say, "Is this the right color?"

She says, "It's fine. Let's go."

"I'm not sure it's at all the right color."

"It's fine," she says again. "Just shut up and stir."

"We need to tape."

"You didn't fucking tape?"

I look at her.

My wife swears a noun, an ugly thing. She throws herself onto the sofa. She is ruddy and damp. Her warm body is twisted on the sofa and hangs loose, pretty. She pushes her hair back from her eyes and sighs, and she swears again. She closes her eyes, and just as I think she has forfeited her interest, she shakes her head and says, "To hell with it." She hops up again and takes my brush, thrashes it through the roller dish.

"The carpet!"

She is deaf and she is dumb. She is swiping at the chair rail in long, reckless strokes. She's made a speckled rill of Green Rill on our old berber. She's crouching like a catcher, raking along the wall next to the fireplace walls. Paint is flinging and dripping. She strokes in those long, reckless strokes, lavishing the wall above and below the rail. Her muscles tremble and twitch. Her knees crack. I take a glob in the forehead and come to. The small of her back.

I have lost my breath.

I haven't really ever seen her like this. She turns and takes my hand, yanks me toward her, kisses me, her tongue firing into my mouth. "C'mon," she pants. "Get into it." Those walls that had kept me up at night are done in thirteen minutes. In thirteen minutes I'm on my back panting beside my wife looking. We're both breathing out of our mouths, leaning against the sofa. It's a whole mess we have here. However, in the public sense, it is done.

Or, as my wife puts it, "It's started."

*

Later, the nooks of the fireplace wall have filled like lake locks. My wife and I are strewn across the floor like castaways, drunkards. She lies flat, draping her arm over her eyes. Her cheeks are red. She swears again. She asks me if I smoke. We laugh. We are utterly wasted. We are glowing. She says, "Could you do more?"

"Right."

She looks up at me. "Seriously."

I am thirty-four years old. I am a little bit nauseous.

*

Later, it's Tuesday evening, and we are stripped down again and going at it like reckless teenagers, like we are doing something lewd that needs to be done very lewdly, very quickly. The windows are done in ten minutes. The cat has Country Rill paws. We laugh.

The laugh is not, as it had been on Monday, robust.

I say, "Do you like it? Is this something you're liking?" I shake my head. "I mean, are you glad we're doing it?"

"It's fine."

"Is it the color?"

"No. It is what it is." She scratches her cheek. "It is what it is. But it's good." She is not telling me the truth. She cannot tell me that if she were able she would just do it all herself. I cannot be obviated, because the project is too enormous for one person. Science hasn't yet really come this far. Not to the Midwest anyway, not to the suburbs and the middle class. It is the contract we'd agreed to, for better or worse, that I be included here. All this is sticky-noted across her face, and then, because she knows that I am reading this, she rolls on the floor and laughs affably.

∗

The first thing we see at the Engelvedts' is their trim. It's running up and down every room in the house. Every damn inch of their house blinds us—finished and lovely color, matted color, glossy color, the shadows of work completed and past, distant hardships. In tremendous insult, they have even sanded away some of their color for a look of fashionable oldness. The kitchen stings with what I'd seen called Icicle spreading above their tall cabinets, just a subtle flourish, but it's there plainly enough to gall. The bathroom has crown molding the color of mud. I have my eyes shielded through half the visit. At dinner, I compliment their attention to detail. "Really," I say.

Bob says, "Really?"

I push the matter. I want to know how long it took them. How long did they have to work, wait. "Give me a ballpark."

Years, for them.

*

I suggest we take a day off on Wednesday, a day away from the painting. It's clearly become a mechanical thing, a means to an end, and is in no way enjoyable. This should be enjoyable, right? Everyone says it should be fun, right?

*

And we finish off the master on Wednesday night. And we shower together, and my wife says, "We have to do a second coat, you know," and she waits for my expression and says, "We aren't done, little buddy," taking my penis in her hand. "We have the rest of the week to do more. We still have Thursday, Friday, Saturday, Sunday, and maybe even Monday morning. We need to get as much paint in there as possible—as much as we've got, as much as you'll get, we need to get it up there." And she calls me little buddy and tells my penis not to pretend he didn't know all of this when we started painting. Because nobody likes a forgetful little buddy.

*

Thursday, we paint, I think.

*

Friday, the brush is frayed and starchy, limpid and stiff at the same time—caked in a sort of translucent lacquer and generally incapable of offering a stroke of Country Rill that does not somehow ruin a previous stroke. My whole rhythm is off. I'm doing harm. My wife just winces, says things like, "Oh Guud." I have covered the kitchen walls three times over. My arms ache, and my hands are blistering badly. I picture my shoulders as the inside of a rotting boat on a destitute beach. I drink water like a dog. I've taken to eating M&M's again. I'm taking down the big bags from megastores that require paid memberships.

I have no idea where my wife is by Friday—

She's glassy eyed across the dining room table from me. Our dinners are fast food, delivered, frozen. When we drag ourselves to the dining room table we no longer pray, no longer regard one another, no longer speak. Anything that does come out of our mouths has to do with the painting—and it's all bad news—and we bite it off the instant it materializes, without our consent or wishes, so that neither of us has to hear that which is bothering our heads in silence. I say on Saturday a.m., "Well?" She shrugs.

*

Who am I kidding? The house and its paint will always be hers. It will always reflect most on her. No one's damning me for anything in this labor. I apply myself.

*

I say I'm going running on Saturday afternoon. My wife raises her eyebrows, questions of where this energy will suddenly be discovered appearing on her brow. It isn't being discovered; I am lying to her. I take the car instead to the store where we were agitated by the rough worker, because they are hosting a free painting clinic there from eleven to two, and I have seen this in the paper at some point, and the rough woman stands in the middle of a square countertop unit that is mounted by at least five cash registers on all sides, and I cannot believe how many people have come to hear her speak.

I can only imagine what things must be like for these others to have brought themselves to this lowness. I came because I did not expect this woman to be the person sawing off advice.

The rough lady goes on and on and on about paintbrushes, concluding that of course no brush is actually any better than what you ultimately do with whatever brush you have. She moves then to paint itself and paint cans and paint types and concludes with the exact same premise, that all paint is the same, insofar as it depends on what you do with the paint you have.

The other customers—geese—are nodding and pecking frantic notes in ink on their palms. I am about to leave when I hear her say something I take with me out the sliding doors near Floral: "Once you start painting, you can never really stop it. Painting is a snowball."

∗

My wife breathes deeply. "I don't know," she says. The clouds outside are bursting, and when all has been cleared and touched up by late, late Sunday, when at last everything is shoved away into the garage and vacuumed and clean and finished, we hold each other, hold each other so tightly I have my wife's rib in my hand. She is trembling and hot, and we can see plainly that we can see nothing clearly. That's it. The color is there, but it exists now as its own thing, unrelated to us.

The rest is up to everyone else, we guess. We guess we have done our part. We guess the time after will be worth the time before.

# LOCAL ACCIDENT

A truck just hit a woman in our neighborhood. The woman lived, but her baby was pronounced dead at the hospital. There were witnesses. They have yet to catch the driver. Many believe he will be found and sentenced, though the incident occurred at night and not one witness can provide a coherent set of details consistent with the details of other witnesses. For days now this event has sobered everyone in the neighborhood. We have brought dolls and candles to the intersection. We have wept and shared stories. We have sung, held and hung signs damning "the coward" who could not face his accident.

In fairness to the specifics of this tragedy, I have yet to mention to anyone that I myself have hit two people with my car before. Neither person died, just as our neighbor did not die, but I hit them both on the same day and both were very much deliberate acts. I hit one of them at exactly 8:30 a.m. and the other shortly after the lunch hour. They were both male. It was the end of the spring. I was very busy. I had many errands. My mind was, as they say, awash.

The first man went up the hood, then down; I clipped the other one and sent him into a dramatic spin. In both cases, I stopped and got out. I did not flee the scene. I could have. I had time. I definitely gave it consideration. How many decisions you can squeeze in a moment! Rather, I stepped out of my car and helped each gentleman—because this is how it's done—off the ground.

Both victims were my bosses. My program director said, "You know, a more detailed explanation would really help me see your side of this a lot more clearly." Then he closed his eyes and told me he needed to sit. He walked away and sat down on the curb. He is a poet, bald, and goes by three names. I let him sit there in silence. He had his head in his hands. I got back in the car and pulled away from the edge, turned off my blinkers, rolled right past him.

My dean is also bald but he always wears a black Orvis Stetson. He insists we address him by his title and his abbreviated first name—Dean D. He popped back up after his dramatic spin and said he was "fine," "excellent," and "this sort of thing happens to the best of us." He was bleeding from the mouth. His knees were exposed through the shreds of his pants. He was very friendly. He dusted me off, swiping at the front of my shoulders. He nodded. He adjusted his hat. I just looked at him. He laughed. I put my hand on his cheek. "Let's call it a career," he said, "shall we?"

After helping him across the street to his office, I got back in my car and drove home. I played ball with my son that afternoon. I remember it well. At eighteen–nineteen in what had become an uncharacteristically physical contest, he received one free throw because we were in the one-and-one bonus. If he'd made the first, he would have received a second and probably carried the game. But the boy missed his first free throw, I wiped that shit off the glass, and I spun elbows-out and called him a "tool" to his face.

He did not care for this. It was too much. He walked away.

I dropped the ball, called after him—another, uglier name. I followed him. I didn't let up with the name-calling. Then I jogged abreast of him and asked him where the hell he was going. He wouldn't speak to me. He sprinted ahead. I watched him run. It was not nice to watch. He's athletic enough, but when he's upset he hobbles like an old lady, all frail hunch and wobbles.

But I knew we were going to the grocery store because my son loves the grocery store. He's drawn there, magnetized by it, by what I don't know exactly, but it's obviously linked to the affair I was caught organizing with a woman there about six years ago. That affair didn't end well for me, our family, or the community at large. Whenever I come in to the store now, everyone looks up, drops their eyes, and shakes their heads. Whenever he comes in, by contrast, they embrace him with a false warmth and familiarity usually reserved for caricatures of Southern domestic life.

I found him sitting in Bread, gagging on Vünder-crüst. I sat down in front of him. The linoleum was cold. "Look," I said, "let's not dick around. This is about your hypothalamus, and you know it. My first time was in a grocery store, actually. Let me tell you about it."

He stopped crying and started to laugh. I could still make him laugh, after all those years, all the injurious behavior of my past.

"I'm sorry I called you those names," I said.

"Do you really believe in repentance?" he asked me.

"I'm not sure trash-talking is really a sin, buddy." But I was thinking about the men I'd struck and nearly killed earlier that day. There is no way he could know, I remember thinking. I tore open the softer Vünderbüns and handed him one. "Atonement," I said and winked, "is way better with starch."

He said, "I'm pregnant. Mary and I are pregnant."

"Okay," I said.

"And Elsa. I'm also pregnant with Elsa. I have two girls pregnant."

There are various ways to experience accidents. There must be. I cannot know if "the coward" designed to strike the pregnant woman, as I had designed to strike my employers. I don't know for certain the role of premeditation in the experience of accidents. Personally, I found the experience a little flat. I'd expected more. I expect my son expected more also. I stood up and walked to the front of the store.

I pulled the display propane grill into Bread. I cranked it. I nabbed some franks from the outskirts of Produce and began rolling them across the grates with a chopstick. My son just sat there at the base of the grill. I ate seventeen hot dogs in about one hour of silence; my son ended up eating half of one. "One thing I know," I finally said to him, when all the food had been eaten. "You are permanently in the bonus and can shoot two free throws for any foul in the indefinite future." He looked wan.

"Look," I said to him. "The fact is you don't always choose your choices. You don't always choose your victims and you don't always choose your witnesses. That's why we call them accidents."

He nodded. "I don't know what that means."

"You're young."

"You're not mad?"

The way the bald poet's head hit my hood reminded me, in that moment, of the way I have from time to time tried to put a glass down on a shiny granite countertop: misjudging the distance, I bring the glass down too quickly and the impact surprises me into violent recoil. And of Dean D. in his dramatic spin: who was that ice skater who, in the most recent Salt Lake Olympics, flung herself through the open doorway during warm-ups, one minute spinning and the next minute—just gone?

I couldn't answer him. I just used my hand to indicate it was time to leave. He stood up. I put my arm around him. I left the grill and the packages right there in the aisle. The people in the grocery store warily watched us leave. We walked home. At some point as we walked, he asked me again if I was angry. "Are you going to kill me?"

The timing and phrasing of this question felt heavy. "I don't like that word," I said.

"But you're not talking."

"Talking isn't the only way to talk," I said.

After a moment, he said, "I don't know what that means."

I let him think about it. I said nothing more.

To the best of my knowledge, my son maintains a friendship with the women with whom he had children at fourteen or fifteen. He may well provide for them emotionally and financially. I don't know. Presently, I believe he is married to another woman, a woman I have only briefly met, and he has four children with her now. They all live in rural Sweden, in a cottage with her parents, according to the post-cards he sometimes sends. He still flies back here to visit his other children in the Madison area from time to time, and the mothers of these other children are married to other men, and they have other children with these other men, of course.

In what I think is the most painful twist in this whole story, the woman who was hit by "the coward" joined us one night at the intersection after she'd been released from the hospital. It was evening, and I don't think anyone expected to see her come up behind us. We were finishing a song, a religious hymn I believe, and many of us were crying quietly to ourselves. "Hi," she said.

We did not turn to look at her. We had no idea it was her! I'm not sure we really heard her until she began to thank us. "This is just so overwhelming," she said.

The sun was setting over her shoulder. It was very bright, piercing, very hard to see her clearly. Most of us were shielding our eyes and squinting as we looked in her direction. Cars were honking through the intersection, so it was difficult to hear everything she was saying. She seemed to be accounting for her recovery, her health, and her gratitude. "But I think it's time to move on," I heard her say suddenly. "We've mourned the dead, and I ask that we all now, for the sake of my husband and my other three children, and family and friends, try to embrace the living and celebrate the life we have together."

Everyone, I could see, was nodding. Everyone, I could see, was lying. Another song was started, and then she eventually left. She just slipped away while we stood there and continued to sing and pray and protest. It was all very hurtful. I think she had no idea the impact she'd had on our lives. I give her the benefit of the doubt, because I have been on both sides of an accident before, but she damn well better believe we deserve more than this.

# SCANDAMERICAN DOMESTIC

The children wanted me to buy them diapers. It was at first silly. Then they voiced up. I couldn't follow their logic; I rejected the appeal. I explained they were not in charge. I told them their silliness wasn't welcome. I may have called them idiots. I may have said they were acting like idiots. It's hard to remember. I definitely told them it wasn't personal. Still, they wept. Every friendship has a bad patch.

I let things cool down. We drove home. I had a cocktail. Then, before bed that night, I kissed the older one on his head. I said I was sorry about earlier, I'd take them to Sweden in the morning. The children leapt from their sheets. We tucked them back in. We shushed them. We hit the lights. My wife's eyes were white flags in the dark room. We closed their door. We went downstairs to speak.

In the kitchen, we did not speak. We shrugged a
lot. I took a blanket back up to the children's bedroom for a sleepover. Sometimes you can spend too
much time with friends, and somewhere over
Greenland I resented my two friends. They were
tearing each other apart. The boy wanted to blow
up his sister. I tried to call my wife: in this modern
day and time, some ten thousand feet closer to
heaven, no service.

I shouldered my unconscious friends through
Stockholm's customs, currency exchange, and bag-
gage. I took a cab directly to an ABBA remake off
Sveavägen. My friends woke to "Waterloo." We
rocked. We soared. The sun never set, at least not
for as long as we were awake, and it felt, we agreed
over a bowl of milkless muesli the next morning,
like we were players in a band dream, a bad band
dream. We laughed into hiccups. Then we passed
out on top of one another and woke up violently ill.

The concierge called an ambulance. We were
wheeled through the lobby. We were studied. We
ate intravenously behind thin and flimsy curtains
for a day. The children were bored: where the hell
is Mommy, anyway?

We returned to the hotel in the off-pink light of four a.m. the next day. I dumped my friends in their big hotel bed. I called down again to the concierge. I asked if it would be hard at this time of the morning to find someone to watch the sleeping children while I went out. In Stockholm, the concierge said, nothing is cheap.

The babysitter he sent up was a delightful man about my age, spirited and amiable. He wore a suit. He said he looked forward to seeing me on my return and if, he leaned toward me, if you are to have a companion with you when you return, I will slip out quietly, no need to fuss. I said I'd like him to be my friend. He said, That's extra. I said, Really? He said, I think we are misunderstanding one another in translation.

I left. I stood in the hallway outside our hotel door. I just stood there. Then I went back in. I released the nice babysitter. I went to the room and woke my friends again. I had to really shake them. This is the time of your life, I pleaded. For godsakes, the days don't get any better than they are right now. Do not sleep this away.

They sobbed. I carried them through the lobby again, and this time I took them to a bar made of glass, shaped like an igloo. It was approximately six degrees inside the igloo. I spilled all my kronor on the crystalline counter and drank all the Svedka this would afford—two shots. At some point the kids began dancing, sliding across the smooth floor in their footies, steam puffing off their heads. I kept drinking ice water. The business lunches started. We were asked to leave.

We plopped down on the street corner.

We talked about their mother, my tentative wife. They said she would have enjoyed this. They said they would have enjoyed their lives more had she been there. They said they wanted something to eat. They said they wanted somewhere to sleep. They said they wanted peace restored to their existence. I told them we all wanted something. I assured them this was not personal.

# DIRECT ASSAULT
# FROM SOUTH SWEDEN

**O**ur son used to draw and color and repeat, "Is this me?" But he was three and behind his peers, we feared. We now understand he was asking us a sincere question. But my wife and I, at that time, we did not see us. We did not see him. We just stared at the paper. He would point to a tiny diagonal slash of crayon ("Is this me?") and we would look at that paper, see nothing, run our fingers through his fine hair, and tell him he was really a wonderful artist.

It's very hard to lie to children. It's also very easy. It gives a person an unpleasing pleasure. But we have so few weapons to tell the truth, we had to lie to him. We clapped and raved and told him we would show his art to various people from whom we would actually hide the art.

We were aware he might march somewhere into the future with this. We talked about it. We said to one another in the coolness of our bedroom sheets that he may never get better at drawing or syntax or anything if we continued lying to him about his shortcomings and inadequacies. We were in agreement that we might never materialize in his eyes and in his life, as our parents had not materialized in our lives, if we kept this up, if we did not push him. And we agreed we might forever find ourselves having to lie to him, as our own parents, as so many people in our families, over the years had lied to us.

So, we pushed him: four times a week, we delivered him to a small house in a fancy neighborhood. The teacher was a lovely woman. She was young. She was someone's daughter. We'd made a few assumptions about her. It was a different era. We were not as progressive and forward-conscious as we now find ourselves. It was true she knew Mandarin, but it was not true that she desired to teach it. She seemed eager to listen to our interest in her language, generally, and very interested in what we were asking her. She smiled so warmly.

(We had stopped her in the grocery store, initially.) We handed her a check and told her, "Please, do what you do," without really clarifying the terms of these sessions except to add, "Just no more art."

But this young woman had no interest in teaching our son Mandarin. She desired instead to teach our son art in English.

I caught them one afternoon in his second year with her. I had been late by about an hour or two picking him up. I'd jogged to the front door of the nice house and knocked. When no one answered, I tell you I became extremely nervous. Some things a parent just *knows,* just *feels.* I went around to the side window and looked in. They were right there at her dining room table. She was reaching across the table, her hand over the top of his. Paper had been scattered, and boxes—huge shoeboxes!—of crayons had been spilled and scattered like a train derailment across the vast mahogany table. He was speaking to her. She was nodding, listening as though he might be offering her counsel.

I rocked that dining room window, I tell you. They both flinched and spun. They looked at me like I was an intruder, an attacker. And then, on recognition, they softened. They waved. My son turned back to her, finished his sentence, and then she looked at me again and signaled for me to go around to the front.

She let me in, greeted me without a smile. She asked if I would like to see my "son's working."

"Let me hear my son speak Chinese."

I moved past her, charged into the dining room. There, in front of the child, was the gun, smoking: a drawing, a person, badly composed. The person was a bubble mess. I could discern the figure's head well enough, yes, and his torso, arms, and legs, but the shape was essentially a colorless and fraudulent attempt at realism. It brought everything back. We had not escaped. We had felt so strongly, so *urgently*, that we needed our son to have something specific and tangible we knew would benefit his future. (We knew the Chinese were going nowhere anytime soon. We knew their language would be extremely "hot" in the coming years of his life. We were no fools! We earnestly, *desperately*, wanted the best for him. And, yes, we wanted him not to blame us for his failures, as we blamed our own families for our failures, and we wanted him not to hold us, as we held our own parents, in contemptuous absentia for the duration of his life. All lost!)

"Say 'hello' to me in Chinese," I demanded.

"Hello," he answered.

"Say 'hello' in Chinese!"

"Hello."

I asked him if he could speak *any* words in Mandarin, and when he could not—when it became clear he had no idea what I was asking him—I just gazed at our young Mandarin teacher until she fled her own dining room in shame.

Oh god—was his heart broken!

He went on weeping without end for days. He spoke in a blubbering we agreed sounded like a foreign language we both knew well. My wife and I nodded: we'd been to this country before. We knew this landscape, this territory, all too well. We knew what it felt like to have your parents undercut, snipe you. We knew what that place sounded like. We knew that language, all right.

And yet, we spurned it. You cannot go around speaking that language. That kind of language will ruin your life prospects. We both knew this, and we told him this, though in different words. "I sounded like my mother," I later reflected to my wife in our cool bedroom sheets. My wife said, "You sounded like my father."

Looking back now, I probably should have told my wife I was trying to persuade the Mandarin teacher to take our son back. I probably should have told her that I had second thoughts, and that I had doubted myself and the brutal and rigid lines we'd drawn for our son's future. The boy had seemed relatively pleasant over those two or three years he'd been visiting the Mandarin teacher's house to indulge his bad art and facilitate the art teacher's fluency in English.

I should have told my wife that I'd been making phone calls and stopping at the woman's house, pleading with her to take my son back. "It would have to be secret," I'd told her. "My wife really can't know about this." I offered to triple her pay. I offered to buy her a new car. I asked her to name her price, name *anything*, and she could have it if she would just take our son back and make him pleasant again.

I should have told my wife all of this, because if I had, I would have discovered sooner that my wife had been doing the same thing. But I could not tell my wife this. It's not easy lying to your wife. I believed our strongest bond was our mutual contempt for the damage our parents had visited on us, and our virulent agreement that we would never allow this damage to be visited on our son. So we would simply rest side by side in bed together in those soft and cool sheets and actively elevate the rhetoric of our love.

"We should forbid the art entirely," I would venture.

"Where can you recycle crayons and markers?"

Things degenerated rapidly in this way. Within that same year we installed the child in a professional for-profit clinic for languages, where he churned out trillions of words for more than two decades. He eventually moved away from us and our small, unassuming neighborhood and married a woman in south Sweden, Malmbäck, the land of our grandparents.

Well, it sure as hell seems that he chose Sweden, particularly south Sweden, to spite us. It feels very much like a direct assault, I can assure you. We feel assaulted, at any rate. Not that he would care. He lives there still, as does this Swedish woman's family we have never met. (We were not invited to the wedding. He told us in an e-mail that he thought it *särskild* the invitation would have been lost in the mail.) They have four children, apparently. We have seen no pictures of his family. We have not seen one of these grandchildren. All we have now, we have stuck to our refrigerator. We still look at those thin lines he used to draw. The paper has faded.

Not that it changes anything, because nothing can diminish the assault our son has campaigned against us, just as we have carried on assaults against our own parents and families, our worst nightmare, but one night not long ago, looking at these pictures on the refrigerator, I said, "Is this me?" And my wife, wrenching her neck, said, "What did you just say?"

It doesn't change anything now to know what he meant then. We know we are what we were.

# TIME IN NORRMALMSTORG

*Akin to what an infant feels when he gets attention,*
*relieving his thirst, hunger, wetness or fear of neglect —*
*a primitive gratitude for the gift of life,*
*an emotion that eventually develops and differentiates*
*into varieties of affection and love.*
— FRANK M. OCHBERG,
ON STOCKHOLM SYNDROME

We attend a party for a five-year-old the size of a
fifteen-year-old and receive long sabers and plastic
pistols at the door. There is our three-year-old with
an eye patch; there's our four-year-old in a black hat
with a wooden sword sticking through it. We all
four come through the busy house, walk out to the
backyard. We stand there looking at other people's
children striking each other, falling, dying, and still
being struck as they lie on the ground already dead.
And then they also shoot one another with their pistols. "This looks challenging," my wife says.

"Can we hit people?" our four-year-old asks.

"Just run for your life," I say.

There is the birthday boy's father brandishing his own, real sidearm for a few of the older children, presumably siblings or relatives of the birthday boy. They are all huddled around this man, and he catches me gaping. It's not loaded, he assures me. I nod. I thank him for that. He is an enormous and hulking man. He is keeping his gaze on me. Even as he speaks to these children about the way in which a bullet can run through one's bone, ricochet through more bones and body tissue and, as his friend once experienced apparently, out the bottom of one's foot into the earth, his eyes keep flashing up at me. My wife leans over and says she doesn't understand what's happened to suburban Madison. Then she walks away. The man is still looking at me. He lifts his chin. I give him a thumb and follow my wife.

One of the birthday boy's relatives has somehow procured a full-scale sailing vessel and had it beached on this back lawn. This is the real deal, a real schooner, I think, two full masts and all the complex rigging. Its hull is enormous. The children look like dwarves running around, killing one another beneath it. The breeze just slightly shifts the tattered sails and the powerful thrum this creates is a stunning whorl you feel in your chest. Our three-year-old is being prevented from going up the ship's rope ladder by large, surly girls standing along the wooden gunwale some twenty yards above her; our four-year-old has somehow ascended the ladder and is now walking the plank, a sword in his spine. "Defend yourself!" I shout. He jumps from twenty yards, plummets screeching, hits the large inflatable mattress rolling, screams, and runs away in tears.

Then the sun changes angles and a piñata materializes. The smoldering grill has been rolled aside, and the children who were still eating at the tables beneath the oaks have been asked-ordered to go sit down on the grass so the piñata can be struck without impediment. The large boys tumble forward with their sabers and the first one squares up. He swats at the thing several times. He is exhausted and falls to his knees. Everyone is standing around with a cocktail. It's nice outside. When the child makes a fool of himself, there's a warmth and mirth about it.

The piñata is a star; it's a perplexing choice. I say to a couple standing next to us that a lot of people wouldn't appreciate the long history of the pirates, the Mexicans, and the Jews. They raise their eyebrows. I nod at them. "It's kind of cool," I say.

I smile at my wife. "Please," she tells me.

Our four-year-old has been cowering for quite a long time in the shadows of his peers, deeply uneasy about all this striking. He has been sniffed out by the bulky father in charge of the piñata and shepherded against his will to stand up to the star and beat it with a stick. It won't be long before he's being told to reach for the stars. He's fascinated by space travel, though it wasn't long before this event that he was terrified of the science museum. Then he became fascinated by the science museum and space travel. Then he began drawing space shuttles and reading books about novas and constellations. And now he is being asked to strike a star.

"Give it the A-Rod," the man says.

My son asks him why.

"It'll make sense after you hit it," the man tells him.

Our child takes the stick, and his first swing is more of a fairy godmother's magical tap of a wand on the very tip of the star's point. Silence grips the performance. Everyone is watching. No one knows what to say. "What a nice boy," wouldn't quite work. His three-year-old sister, who is watching her older brother, shouts, "Kill it!"

But he is four and tender, and he's been told not to strike anything as recently as that morning, and he's said he *understands* this, and perhaps he really does—because he begins to crumble. I open my mouth. My wife steps forward. But the bulky father snatches the stick from my son's hands and says, "Like this, son." He pushes my son back, stands tall, throttles the star so hard it flings off its twine tether and lands in the neighbor's yard several hundred feet away.

My son is stunned by this. He hasn't even seen where the star has gone. It's just gone, vanished, a magic trick. He laughs and cries at the same time.

And then later that night we are in bed—all four of us—discussing the value of our day. The three-year-old wants to know what *killing* is; the four-year-old wants to know what it means to *A-Rod*. I explain

that piñatas are naughty and tend to bring out the
worst in everyone. "So do pirates and parties and
weapons," my wife says. I nod with her. The children,
however, laugh. They understand that this makes no
sense. This is when my daughter takes the book she's
holding and swings it into her brother's face.

She connects spine with eyeball. Before our
son is screaming, there is silence, a broad sucking
of air from the room. And then he is wailing,
thrashing about in the bedsheets. We tend to him.
The three-year-old is screaming, terrified at the
work of her own hands. We reprimand her. She
says *stand* before we can even get the word *under*
out of our mouths, which means she probably will-
fully rejects understanding what she's done. Or it
means she understands everything perfectly well
but cannot tolerate reconciling what she understands. I pull her aside, sit her down, and ask her
again if she really understands—and she *stands* so
quickly I can't even get the *d* off the back of my
teeth. I tell her to look into my eyes. I tell her to
look at my face. My wife comes over and asks her
if we look like we think this is funny. We ask her if
she would like to be hit in the face with a book. We

ask her if she would like to be injured. She says she would not.

We let this end the discussion. We bed them. We shut off the lights. We demand *silence* until morning. We go downstairs. I start a glass of wine. My wife goes to the bathroom. Then I pour my wine into the sink and fill the wine glass with gin. I pick up the phone and call the father of the pirate boy-man whose party we attended. I tell him about my night. I ask him if he's worried about breeding violence in a world already rocked by so much violence, hatred, mistrust, and rage.

He's silent on the other end. He gets what I'm after. "They're five," he says.

"Mine are three and four."

"Do you want me to apologize?"

"I need to think about it." I hang up.

Then he calls back and asks if I could give him a lesson on raising kids like female genitalia. I call him the name for male genitalia and ask if he'd like his lessons over the phone or in person. We meet an hour later at the McDonald's on the corner of Main and University. It would have been about eleven at night. I have no idea how I got there. I have no memory of grabbing my keys, driving there. I have no memory of waiting at stoplights, listening to something on the radio. I remember seeing him step out of his silver Range Rover. I remember going over to him, facing him, and then coming home in a police car.

I am beaten so badly the police say they couldn't even describe me as having been involved in the disorderly conduct charge leveled against the other boy's father. They want to call an ambulance, but I plead my poverty and insist my wife will take care of me and keep me safely locked up in the prison of our home. The next thing I remember is meeting my wife at the front door with the police officer. She covers her mouth with her hand as she looks at me standing there.

"He had a big pipe," I say.

"Those were his hands," the officer says.

My wife takes me by the shoulder and hugs me. She tells the officer I have psychological damage that even the doctors don't understand.

*

At Early Childhood Education on Monday morning, I walk past the five-year-old birthday boy and his mother. She smiles at me. I thank her for the party.

"I'm good," she says.

I nod.

"How are *you*?" She is smiling. "I've been worried about you."

"I have reason to be worried about you too."

"Oh," she says, "he treats me like a princess."

I touch the stitches above and below my right eye. "Me too," I say.

She laughs.

I think this is flirting. I go with it. I flirt with her for the better part of ten minutes. She is touching my face and shaking her head. The teacher of our children is looking at us. She comes over and asks what happened to me. The birthday boy's mother tells her that her husband kicked my ass. "Absolutely destroyed me," I say. They laugh. We are all laughing.

Later that afternoon, an e-mail is sent to the parents of the class asking for donations to cover the cost of my medical bills. The e-mail details the night of the fight, the specifics of what her husband did to me, and makes the urgent plea that while my family "may have the bills covered at present for the superficial injuries," there is no telling the number of injuries that may have "latent manifestation—brain and emotional injuries, primarily."

"Is this supposed to be funny?" my wife says when she reads it.

"I really don't know."

My wife doesn't find it funny. "It appears the woman is trying to make you look like an idiot."

"It would appear," I say.

My wife suggests I go over to their house and talk about this with them. She suggests that, despite the clear success of my hostile engagements with this family, I might try something less obvious: like human reason.

I nod. I am not optimistic. I am married.

And the streets of our Madison suburb on this Monday afternoon are a lesson in the sublime. They are sprawling hilly blocks of sweeping plots of lawn without sidewalks. One is kept on the street at all times if one is not on a driveway. I find this forced distance between the street and the houses flatters the houses in a false way. It's true of our own house: the closer you get, the less remarkable the house becomes, the more you wish you were still standing down on the street looking up to admire it.

Moreover, the distance between the houses is deceptive and stunning. By the time you've arrived at the door of your neighbor, which is, as we often like to lie to ourselves, *just down the way,* you're so winded you really can't recall what could possibly have mattered enough to take this walk in the first place. In turn, very few people walk through our sublime. It's untenable. And it's lonely and quiet and eerie. Yet, I know very clearly what I'm doing, why I'm approaching the house of the family that just recently assaulted me.

The five-year-old boy who looks more like a fifteen-year-old man opens the door when I ring the bell. He looks at me. "He isn't home," he says.

"I'm here to talk with both of your parents, pirate."

"Want some lemonade?"

I take a glass from his hand. We sit down on the small step off his front doorway. "I'm bored," he says.

I nod. I ask where his parents have gone. He tells me he doesn't know. I ask him how old he is. "You were at my birthday," he says, "like a few days ago."

I nod. The lemonade is terrible. It isn't lemonade. I don't know what it is. He has made it himself, he tells me. I pour it out. He looks at it streaming down the steps. I apologize. I ask him if he frequently stays home alone.

"I'm not alone," he says.

I look at him.

He asks me what happened to my face.

"Who's home? Is your father at home?"

"My parents aren't here." He reaches to touch my face. I pull away. He tries to touch my face again. I stand.

"Let me touch your stitches."

"No. How are you not alone if no one is here? Is someone here?" He stands up and goes right after my face. I grab his hands in mine. I hold those little hands firmly. They are tiny wrists, even for a large boy. I look him in the face. He is clearly five, maybe four. I have his attention now. He's in some reasonable amount of discomfort in my hands. "They're fucking around in the back," he says.

"They're in the backyard," I repeat. I let his hands go.

He nods. "They'll kill you," he says, "and probably they'll make me eat your testicles for dinner."

I touch his shoulder. "Don't talk like that."

He doesn't say anything.

"Anyway," I clarify, "I'm not here to fight."

He laughs. "Good luck with that." He gives me a thumb over his shoulder.

And then I walk through the enormous entryway to the house and into their grand living space, which is cleaner and more pristine than any living space I've ever seen. I hadn't noticed this at the party, when the house had been bloated with people inside and out. Their living space is a vast and unadulterated hollow, a catalog image. The kitchen is also without blemish, perhaps never used. In the back, through the French doors, I see the schooner that entertained the children at the party. I open the French doors and stand silently a few steps into the yard.

Before I am shot in the shoulder and then directly in the center of my chest, I see the child's mother in a black do-rag and eye patch charging me from behind the ship's rudder. I see smoke and fire rising from her hands and I think, though I cannot be positive, I see she is missing teeth as she is shouting, her face rent in expressions of contempt. And she is approaching me in full sprint until I can no longer see her. The impact of the gunshots has delivered me, strangely bent and generally without feeling, to the lawn. A man is above me. His face is upside down. He is speaking to me. I take his hand and, just before he strikes the bridge of my nose with the hilt of a glinting saber, I think I may not have been shot after all, may have imagined it. Then I'm on my back again. I feel my nose pressing against my eyeball and my lip is sneering, the wind brushing the gums along my upper teeth. It crosses my mind with more certainty and clarity now that I have been shot and that these people are attacking me and that I am in danger. I cannot move my extremities. I cannot see for a liquid altering my sight.

The man's boot is in my crotch, I can vaguely make out, but I don't feel this. He is standing on me with both boots. There's pressure without feeling. Then the woman's face appears again with the black aperture of her gun in my one working line of sight. Then it's dark. Then there's a pressure loud enough to ring like the highest-pitched weeping of my scarlet-faced child, who I am next seeing in dull purple, and she is a lovely face, just three, but she has my hand in her hands. She is saying to me, looking right at me, "Dad, we're just screwing with you. We get it. We totally understand. We totally *stand*. We know right from wrong. It's just more fun to see the way you hate wrong." And then she laughs and helps me to my feet.

And then I am standing on the street again, just at the edge of the driveway to the man-boy's house. He is standing on the step to his house, waving at me. "What happened to your face?" he shouts. I wave back and head toward what I believe to be my home. I take some comfort in the walking home. Cars slow down as they pass. I wave. It's a good feeling, and it's quiet. I can hear the wind. I can hear people speaking in distant rooms of these large houses that are set way back on enormous beds of lawn—lawn that feels only less soft than it appears. And sometimes I lie down. Sometimes I think about someone covering me with a blanket. But no one stops their car, and no one sees me. So, sometimes I get up and continue home, and sometimes I sit back down and think about what I would have said had the boy's parents not attacked me. Sometimes I say to the father that he can live his life any way he chooses. I tell him I respect him. I tell him I respect violence and general meanness as a legitimate way of life. Sometimes he asks me what the hell I am talking about. "It's cool," I say. "We're cool." Sometimes I say, "That's cool, you're cool." "Thanks," he says, and he turns his vacuum cleaner back on, because he has been vacuuming his tool-shed, and I say there are greater weapons than pipes and candor is one of them. But he cannot hear me and he doesn't say anything else to me. Sometimes he shuts off that vacuum cleaner and comes over and shakes my hand. And sometimes he comes over and tries, were I not so svelte, quick, and dexterous, to knife me with a small dagger he draws from his sock.

Through the windows of the houses people appear to be changing clothes, stirring things in pots on stoves, standing and looking at things I cannot see through their walls. My feet press gravel. My mouth opens and shuts. I feel the wind on my teeth. I believe I may be crying. As I near our home, I can hear the yelling of my children through the windows.

They are in time-out again. I check my watch; it is four in the afternoon, or it is ten in the morning. The dial is moving strangely, perhaps broken. I close the door behind me after I come in, and I lock it. Brutality can do the work of a million words: my children are struck dumb, finally. Finally, the children are silent. Finally, they understand something.

*

And then I hear my wife gasp, and the rest of that year and through the holidays I am in hospitals and police rooms and courtrooms. I sleep frequently. I sleep upstairs in our house on a long chair designed to comfort my healing, and I listen to the children's mother asking them if they under, and they do, they stand, and they are told to whisper. The Christmas tree comes and goes, as do the white lights, and the days become shorter and then longer through the windows upstairs. A bad cold enters me and leaves me in February, but I am feeling well enough in March to come downstairs. My wife is at the kitchen sink. The children are in time-out. They have destroyed one another's fairy castles. Dolls are cast across the floor, victims of some marauding. I take my wife in my hands, and I tell her I am sorry.

She says she is sorry. I say I am sorry, again. We hold, and it is stunning how clunky it feels to kiss at our age, how bad we've become at something as basic as this.

And still, somehow, there's something potential and volatile there. We kiss again and the press of our bodies is warming and important. She smiles and says, "Later." I tell her I like this idea of *later*. It's the first time I can remember saying something not thoughtless in a long time.

"Listen," my wife says, "I need to tell you something."

I think we are going to talk about something sexual, and I fall into listening to discover that she has been in contact with the boy's parents, the people who tried to kill me for sport. They are still awaiting their trial. "They're really embarrassed," she says.

"Embarrassed," I repeat. But this is Madison, where *embarrassment* is tantamount to *raped*. We feel unspeakably bad toward those who are embarrassed. It's more painful to see a neighbor embarrassed than the dead in an open coffin. My wife means to say they are racked by the weight of public guilt and remorse and shame. I know this. She knows I know this. "They're actually good people," she tells me.

I really don't know what to say. So I say, "Did they call us, or did you call them?"

"They called you, it turns out. They walked over the day they posted bail. This was even before they picked their own son up from social services. I think we should have them over for dinner."

"I think that's a really good idea," I say.

She says, "It's the right thing to do."

"I think we should probably have them hung."

She nods. "Sounds like you're ready to be an adult."

"Sounds like you're ready to be an idiot." This postpones the inevitable for a few more months, until a few days before their sentencing date, when my wife proposes it again. We have already communicated to our lawyers that the only charges we want to press are the ones that will cover the medical costs. Our lawyers just shake their heads. My wife says, "We only have a few more days to make this gesture. After the trial, it'll seem more awkward."

She is probably right. And the children are so annoying, and I have been alone in this house with

these people for so many days and months I'm finding myself curious to see what embarrassment looks
like on someone else.

And then they arrive with a bottle of cheap wine
and a casserole. Their giant son charges through the
door and immediately lunges on top of my daughter.
The mother lunges at me with an embrace, and it
appears she has been crying. Her breath is whiskey.
She holds me and kisses me on the cheek—and then
on the eyes and my other cheeks. She is saying she
is so sorry. Her husband is laughing as he hugs my
wife. Then his wife releases me, and he and I face
one another as we did briefly that night in the
McDonald's parking lot. We laugh, and then we
embrace. I confess a powerful feeling swelling in my
face. I have to look away to avoid letting him see me
cry. But I know he is not crying, nor is he close to
crying. "Got the game on?" he asks me.

It is May. I have no idea what game he could be
referring to. I tell him I just turned it off. "That's
cool," he says. We walk into the living room amid all
the toys. He seems unaware of the toys as he steps
right on top of them, crushing the Duplos and
smashing my son's small cars into the carpet. He

compliments my ceiling. "I love ceilings," he says. He reaches up and touches it, runs his hand along the plaster. "Fuck," he says, "that's nice."

The women have gone to the kitchen, as I suppose they feel they must, and I sit down with this man and ask him how things have been going. He looks at me squarely. "Business has been hotter than hell," he reports. "I'm making a killing in commercial right now."

I nod.

He tells me I wouldn't know it from the news, but people are buying commercial like it's going away sometime soon. He laughs. "That shit isn't going anywhere except in my pocket!"

I thank him for coming over. I look into the hallway to see his son standing there looking at me. The boy is smiling at me; then he approaches and stands about three feet away from me. I smile at him. I look at his father. "I haven't had a good conversation about real estate in so long," I tell him.

He says, "What's the point if you're not in the business?"

"That's reasonable," I say.

"What happened to your face?" the boy asks.

I say to his father that I've always felt the empty strip malls in Middleton were a gold mine of opportunity.

He laughs in such a way that spit flings off his lips. "Shit gold," he says. "Those places sit on a septic field ten miles long."

"That explains that."

The child has edged even closer. He has his hand extended and I lean back. His father is still admiring our ceiling. "I'd like these in my garage," he says.

"Easy, pirate," I say to the boy.

"What happened to your face?"

I take the child's hand. "They were very big in the eighties," I say to the father.

He looks at me. I am sure he will address his son now, now that he sees the boy in my hands. "You're fucking me," he says.

"I think it was the eighties," I say. I am just staring at the child now, straight in the eyes. I say to the father, "Good-looking kid you've got here."

"Look," the father says. He clears his throat. "Maybe now isn't the best time for this."

"O.K.," I say.

"Maybe we could meet for a drink, because this may not be appropriate."

"O.K."

"I just want you to know that Angel and I have talked about it a lot. We just want you to know where we're coming from."

I make a noise. I nod. I try moving the man's son away from me.

"We know we shouldn't have shot you. We get that. We believe in reality, right? We believe in being real."

"O.K." I have to look at him over the top of his struggling child. This boy is nearly in my lap. He has one hand on my thigh, and I am actively staving off his other hand by gripping the child's wrist. I am using a good deal of my strength in this grip, and the child begins to feel the pain. He begins to moan. I release him and he runs to the kitchen.

"Fucking kids," the father says.

"Maybe I should get you a drink," I say.

"You got any port?"

And then, mercifully, within that very breath, we are summoned to the dinner table. I let him stand and go ahead of me. I am to be seated, it appears as

I enter, right beside their enormous child. My wife has placed me near this child, and she has placed our children at the opposite end of the table, near where she'll be sitting. She wants to keep our children away from their children, and I understand this. It's the right thing and best thing for the cycles of evolving humanity. Yet I am the one who is now made to sit beside him. And he goes right to work. "You look like you've had some trouble," he says. "Has someone hurt you?" I look at my wife. She is smiling. I smile. We don't speak. The man-boy repeatedly tries to touch my face, and somewhere during a bite of salad I finally let him.

"You're deformed," he says, running his wet fingers across my nose and my cheekbones. "You've been beaten."

My son asks what it means to *beat*.

"It means nothing," I say.

"My dad isn't deformed," the boy says. "He has scars all on his knuckles." He then asks his father to show us those knuckles, and the father does so.

My children are interested. They look at his fists. My daughter asks what a *scar* is.

"It's a boo-boo," I say.

The man clears his throat.

"We should put Band-Aids on his hands," my daughter says.

This makes me laugh. The boy kicks me. He tries to grab my leg, and he asks again to touch my disfigurements.

Apparently becoming aware that I am not at ease, the mother of this child, Angel, repeats what the husband has already told me about their belief in reality, in being real. She says this in a very concerned way. She touches her glass while she talks. She nods softly to herself as she explains a stance no one solicited. "We just believe in accepting the consequences of a savage and unkind world."

My wife says, "That's nice."

"Yeah," the woman says. "I guess I've always believed that in a world like this one, you have to pay to play."

My wife and I nod. We are certainly paying.

"If you aren't willing to pay," she continues, "you aren't ready to play."

I say, "We're definitely paying to pay, yes."

"Play," the woman clarifies.

"Pay," I say. "I heard you."

"Well," my wife will later say in our bedroom, "I've never been more proud to call you my husband. I've never seen you sexier than you were in your restraint. I love the new tame you. The new thoughtful and humane you makes me exceptionally interested in you."

"I'm not sure I'm a fan," I will answer.

And she will say, "I would like to show you some things the old you would never see."

She is a woman of powerful restraint, my wife, and I will follow her whenever she moves toward indulgence. And she will drop her pants and step out of her underpants, and she will lift her T-shirt over her head and drop it at her feet, and she will bend over the bed and tug the sheets off, and she will flip them in the air and spread them on the floor. She will turn to me and take off my shirt, and she will kneel and slide my pants down my legs, and she will tell me to get down on the floor with her, and I will do this, and the machinations of the condom will seem ridiculous, but she will do it for me, and she will do it in earnest, and she will say, Oh god, and she will have those long fingers on me, and she will get down on top of me, and she will say,

Does this hurt you? and she will ask again, Does this hurt you? and I will hear the boy's voice asking me this, "Does this hurt you?"

"Does this hurt you?"

And then the boy's hand is up against my face, patting it, and I don't know where the conversation at the table has gone, but everyone seems to be having a nice time until I take that kid's hand, and I squeeze it, and I twist—and I snap it. Just like that. But it's not what I thought it would be. It's not what you see on television. It's not what you're told. It's not what you expect. The child is loud, screaming. The boy is nearly blue. You really feel for him, it's true. The bone comes right through. The bone is huge. The skin falls back, peels right back and all that's left is this bone sticking out. But it's also so small. It all seems so tiny, like a little chicken bone. And it also feels so just, and I really do, I really do think everyone sitting there looking at one another, I really do think we finally understood one another and what we were all dealing with here.

## WHEN OUR SON, 26,
## BRINGS US HIS FIRST GIRLFRIEND

Our son's departure to college helped. That's a fact. The house went quiet. We had very little to discuss. The amount of sighing decreased. Life slowed to an inching. I swear I could count the staging seconds of the rising sun, and also those of its setting out the other window.

Weekends, the boy would come home, parched. He drank water straight from the spigot, hours on end, replenishing for the coming week.

Fantasizing about my funeral, I would sometimes imagine everyone dry-eyed, rock-faced. I would imagine this—the day of my funeral—is the first day in my son's life he doesn't cry. He'd dump a few of his toy trucks down on my casket and walk on. He'd hug his mother. Arm in arm, they would walk away from the grave and discuss their lunch. He feels full, my son would say to her. He feels a little bloated, truth be told. My wife would say that's funny, because she feels disemboweled.

But because I didn't die, we ended up living for many years in the perpetual horror and guilt of our son's ceaseless crying. His departure to college helped, as I say, but we are parents—we still fretted. *What must his professors think? What a shame to be his roommate, his friend. Who will clean all those fucking shammy cloths?*

Then one weekend in his sophomore year he brings a girl home, a nice girl, very big. She glares at me glaring at my son, a sign of what is to come, but I imagine he finds this wary vigilance of hers soothing. He jags up the crying that night in his old bedroom, just as he's always done. We dip toward sleep until we hear her climb the stairs from the guest room; we hear her slip into his room and tell him he is *such a loser* and if he doesn't *pull his emotional shit together* she'll leave him, *straight up.* How could he expect anyone to *handle his parents* while he does all the crying, all the *stealing of the obvious drama*?

My wife and I look at one another. We smile. We could hear our boy sobbing without restraint at those remarks. It's hard. No one wishes this sort of thing for their child, but we smile.

Then she suddenly apologizes and collapses onto his bed and tells him she was wrong—way, way wrong, how cruel she could be, he brings out in her a personality she had long feared she possessed. We hear silence, and then we hear them making what we recognize must be exceptionally uncomfortable love on his tiny childhood bed, and I fall asleep, for just a few minutes, just a knot of disgust.

—In the sudden darkness I start up again, realizing I can no longer hear our boy crying. It's a Sunday morning, I think, and I don't know what this means, and I look over at my wife and sitting up in the bed, shaking her, tell her *Listen, Listen, Listen, I hear nothing*.

We spent what seemed like years driving around that morning looking for an open ice cream place so we could suckle cold dairy together in celebration. Our baby boy laughed and laughed with his girlfriend, and whenever he stopped laughing, to catch his breath and suck his ice cream, my wife and I froze for an instant, terrified the tears would return.

But that was it. He wouldn't start crying again. I had not died, not literally, and still we had found our way to the day when our boy, at twenty-six, stopped crying. It was enormous. It changed everything. We were no longer guilty of the crimes that had made our son cry all these years. It's unsavory to use the word *relief,* but there it is, and I told my wife I would go back to work again, and I said I would try to be a better person to strangers, and my wife and I had sex again sometime later that year.

# O SWEET ONE IN THE BLUFF

At first I actually *could* speak to her. I could speak to her quite often, actually quite naturally. She just couldn't speak back, and that really helped. I repeatedly told her I was in love with her, every time I saw her rolling on the carpet, ogling the ceiling, anytime I could catch her conscious. "My god," I could say to her then. "I love you so much, my little beautiful sussypants."

And my wife would roll her eyes. "Must be nice," she would say.

But then my daughter started speaking and it was enormous and awesome in its own way. She was twelve, thirteen months old. She manufactured verbal things like "ad" and "non." It was awesome, and the awesome totally silenced me, utterly shut me down again. I went solid stone with her—and sulky.

It was as if I was trying to date again, back on the scene some twenty years later.

I had major problems with dating, as everyone knows, because it's very hard to date when you can't speak naturally to the intended objects of your interest. You have to rely on your body. I have a really good body, really fit, thank god, and everyone knows that if my wife hadn't been into my body and therefore determined to break me socially, back when we were in college, I might have tumbled, silent and abstinent, into my lonely, filthy little grave.

But my wife did break me, thank god.

Or so I thought. For all these years I've been pretty much broken, talking to men and to women with relative comfort, relative niceness. But then we had this daughter of ours, and she wanted to speak to me pretty much as soon as she could begin speaking, and I could not say a thing back to her. At first I *could* talk to her, yes, but this lasted—in the framework of a lifetime—about twenty seconds. My wife absorbed my silence to my daughter as she would a personal injury to herself. She couldn't summon the same determination to break me as she had when we'd been courting. She was wounded by it, hurt, suffering. She cried a lot. She whimpered. She got frustrated and loudly banged things on the counters in bursts of anxiety. And yet she tried to help me. She sat me down across from our daughter and said things like, "Go ahead. Just say, 'Hi.' Just say, 'Hey.' Just start with one word."

I would have to shake my head. I had a rock in my throat. "No."

"Just say the first thing that pops out of your heart," she tried.

"I want to tell her I'm in love with her."

My wife took a breath and looked off to a distant country. "Maybe try something less dramatic."

She was very patient. She is an extraordinary woman. She stood there and watched me staring at my daughter. "Dad," my daughter would later say to me, "play with me." And I *would* play with her. But I would do so in silence. I maneuvered fancy-smelling purple and pink horses into and out of fairylands. I combed her long honey hair. I took her to the swing set, pushed her. I just did it all without voicing a single word to her. I just looked at her. And my wife just looked at me, often agape.

"Either this indicates you're a misogynist," my therapist offered, "a hater of all women, or else you're homosexual and closeted. Perhaps you've transferred your wanton cravings for men into an abject contempt for the natural interest your daughter might have in speaking with you."

My wife offered, "I worry the only thing we talk about anymore is our daughter."

"I sometimes talk about me."

"Yes," she answered quietly. "Let's not do that anymore." So in time I didn't talk to my wife about our daughter, or about anything, and I stopped talking to everyone and entered a phase of comprehensive silence where I was only writing notes down on a piece of paper at grocery stores, to pester a shelving clerk about the new location for the organic produce or something, and I answered the telephone only to hear someone speak to me before hanging up on them. At work, I wrote to my boss and director that I had my tongue severed for religious reasons, and I handed them a copy of my protected rights. I fell into studying my domestic life as a qualitative scientist might study a troubling case: I took extensive notes on my wife's patterns of toiletry usage and tended nightly a three-dimensional scatter chart depicting the angles at which my daughter would prop her cell phone against her face while speaking to different interlocutors—males, females, adults (10–13, 14–16, 17+).

Then one afternoon while my wife was out of the house, my daughter came to me in the kitchen. I was scouring pans. She was unusually fidgety, very pretty. She said to me, "I am a total fuckwaste."

I shut off the water and turned to her. "That is a lie," I said.

"Holy—" she said. She put her hands over her mouth. Then she put them on top of her head. She was smiling. I hadn't seen her smile in more than a decade.

The power of sight is often smothered by its sister senses, especially sound and smell, but I have found sight to be my greatest and closest friend over the years, particularly in my silence. It was our first direct exchange in her cerebral life, and I found the visual dimension of that moment its most gratifying aspect. She had amazing teeth, it turns out, and her cheeks formed dimples that ran clear to her ears. I had never seen that. It wasn't the way her mother had ever smiled with me. Perhaps, indeed, her mother had never smiled with me, a gutting thought.

"I need to get out of here," my daughter repeated.

I nodded.

"My life is about to end," she said. "And I have to get the hell out of here. Let's just go. You don't need to talk. I want to go to the mountain. I'll drive. You don't have to talk or do anything. I just need to go. I just want you to come with me. We can pan for gold, or something, I don't know."

"Do you want me to talk?"

She thought about this for a moment. "No."

She must have seen me sink.

"That's why I asked you and not Mom. I just need someone to be with who won't tell me what to do."

I nodded and rubbed my face. I had a lot I wanted to say that she was making me swallow.

I had never been to the mountain. I had no idea what people did on the mountain. It is the only mountain in Wisconsin. Indeed, it is the only mountain within a one- or two-thousand-mile radius. Indeed, it's not a mountain at all. It's a bluff, and because we see it as a bluff, a total fraud, we call it a mountain. Miners liked it years ago. But that didn't last, and I can see why. It has always seemed a particularly depressing mountain to me. It has always seemed like some ecological flaw, a misstep of creation, an eyesore that suppressed our property values and our perspectives—a painfully slow rising from the earth matched only by its salient and rather unpleasing drop back down again—a metaphor to kill the pleasure of all metaphors in and around and about this countryside.

I probably should have discouraged her from driving. She was fourteen. She passed cars on the right edge of the highway. She played extraordinarily loud music. The music seemed unbelievably unrelatable. I wondered at the calibration of their anger and what a world looked like in which people wore their anger so openly, or a world in which people paid money to hear people so fluent with their anger. I nearly bit my hand off as we rounded the tight switchbacks. I have never been more grateful to see a parking lot.

We left the car and crossed a wooden bridge leading to a prefabricated cabin built off the face of the mountain. I wanted to know how she'd known this place was here, but she would not read my note. She said, "Let's go" like we were actors in some television crime drama. But I kept pace with her, and I remained silent. We paid fifteen dollars each (she paid for herself on a credit card I had not, to my knowledge, cosigned for her) for a flimsy tin lid. The broken-toothed and partially bearded man at the counter said, "He know what he doing?"

"No one knows what they're doing, Billy," my daughter said.

He laughed. His mouth was a gothic cage. "You go like this," he said to me. "Not like this. Got it?"

I nodded. I did not have it. I had no idea what he was talking about. I smelled whiskey, and I wanted a long drink. He pointed us out the back door, which he had propped open, and I could see through the back door another long bridge and a set of stairs that went down to the creek near the base of the mountain. He winked at me.

I followed my daughter. She didn't speak. I didn't speak. It was, by then, late afternoon. The light fell against the face of the mountain rock in a pleasant way, so that I could see the black flies swarming against the pollen and motes. At the bottom of the stairs we went straight for the creek bed. I knelt down.

"Not here," she said.

I stood back up.

She was looking around me, around us, and back up to the prefabricated cabin. Sensing, I suppose, that we were not being watched, she moved quickly up the creek, and I followed. We walked for another twenty minutes until we arrived at the entrance to a mine portal. The entrance was boarded over. The creek was spilling from beneath the boards. She stomped into the water, across the slick rocks, and went directly to the entrance to begin yanking boards away.

I am not great at transgressions, which makes me both a great and horrible father. She seemed to expect that I would not be able to assist her in her violation of mine property, as she did not turn around to ask for help. She grunted; noises I had never heard her make came up from her belly and her heart, and she pulled against a final plank with a yell I *had* actually heard her use before, somewhat frequently, with her mother. But she could not get that last plank away. She turned to me. "Someone used screws."

I made a face. I came over.

Indeed, someone had screwed the planks to the wooden framing of the mine. The screws were new, shiny silver. I put my foot along the side and really yanked. It came off, and I fell heavily onto the rocks and creek behind me.

She ducked down and went in. I scrambled up out of the water and went with her. "Watch your" became the opening of her every sentence inside that mountain. "Watch your head" and "Watch your step" and "Watch your right." I just stayed close to her, following her deeper into the dark. I tried to keep my hand on her back. I tried to thread my finger through the hole of her shorts belt loop, but she was so fast. It's a good thing I have such a nice body, I thought to myself, though I was hunched over and shuffling forward like a witch.

"Tell me your thoughts on dark, damp holes," my therapist said. "You're clearly drawn to holes. You love to talk about them. You have some sort of obsession with them. I'm interested in the type of holes that most fascinate you, call to you, sometimes maybe come to you in your dreams. Because we all have holes, don't we, that we want others to explore? And we know that, as we have holes, so too do others. And we like to look and explore holes to make sure theirs are like our own."

Indeed the mine was dark, and it was wet. But it was cool bordering on cold. It became very dark very rapidly, swallowing any of the late-day's light that had earlier been chasing us. I turned around a few times and saw nothing—literally the portrait of nothing. My daughter used a small keychain flashlight to guide us through the passageways. Its power against this darkness was astonishing. I said nothing.

Then she stopped and shone her flashlight into a stretch of water that appeared clouded by lime and alluvial tailings where the mine had been flooded and simply pooled. She turned to me and put a hand on my chest. "This is where things get a little weird," she said.

I nodded.

"Be ready. I just met her a few weeks ago. She's in some trouble, O.K.? So am I. I'm going to show her to you now. You'll get it when you see her."

I expected a dead child. I don't know why. It might have made more sense, in retrospect, to have imagined an animal or underworld science-fiction creature. But that's what I pictured. I thought of a dead child. "Are you going to kill me?" I said.

She shushed me. "Just think about what we're going to do with this information. Don't worry about what it means. o.k.? And don't talk."

She then turned the flashlight farther up the pool of water, deeper into the mine. I had to squint, but I could see, in the dim and pasty light, a woman looking back at me.

"Hi, Hannah," my daughter said. "It's me."

The woman I could see in the pool, in a bikini, was at once familiar and yet very, very strange to me. She was smoking a cigarette, though I could not smell the smoke. She was sitting on the far edge of the pool of water, her legs submerged to her knees. Her bikini looked to be red and floral. She wore her blond hair long and back, in a bun, and she looked ruddy, with high rosy cheeks, but there was no mistaking that this woman was my daughter, older. I was seeing the specter of my daughter as an adult. She was waving. "Hannah doesn't speak to me either," my daughter said to me, loud enough that it seemed she wanted the woman to hear her.

"How do you know her name is Hannah?"

"Shhh," she said.

"It's you," I said.

She shushed me again, this time with some force. "I know who it is, *Dad*."

Then we stood there in silence. I really didn't know what to say. The woman remained on the other side of the water. We would have to get into the water to go toward her. I presumed that was where this was headed. Or I imagined this woman, this specter of my daughter, would lower herself into the water and swim over to us. But nothing occurred; no person of the three of us moved. My daughter kept the flashlight on this woman and the woman continued smoking.

She had stopped waving, but she looked back at us as though we were in meaningful conversation. She nodded nicely. She shifted every now and then, and I could hear the harsh scratch of the loose mine surface beneath her when she did. Except when she would wince while moving her weight, she remained largely placid in her expression, entirely matter-of-fact.

"Just wait," my daughter whispered to me. "You O.K., Hannah?" she called. "Can I get you anything?"

The woman shook her head and shifted once more. She pulled a leg from the water and the light from my daughter's flashlight caught a surprising angle in her profile. I had not been able to see it before, but it was clear in an instant that this woman was pregnant. Her belly was enormous! She plopped her near hand on her womb. She tipped her head back and looked up to the roof of the mine. She opened her mouth and groaned.

And then the light went out and I stood there stone silent in the dark.

I didn't move. I could see nothing. My eyes failed to adjust to the new light, because the new light was an utter absence of light, something I had never seen before, and something I have never seen since. The image of my pregnant daughter burned and glowed in my head, but if there are degrees of darkness there are surely degrees of silence, and I tell you I left a lifetime of relevant verbal matter stuffed inside that hole no one knows how to mine any longer.

# THE COOK AT SWEDISH CASTLE

The cook was no cook. He had only role-played one at his grandmother's house in Chicago as a boy. Yet flying back for his grandmother's funeral, he found himself entirely preoccupied with playing the cook again. The prospect made his feet throb. Maybe, in the end, there was nothing larger than the cook. Even sitting in the pew, silent and solemn before the service, Able could not shake the trembling.

And then his mother's sister roped her arms around his neck and asked him if he would say a few words. "You are always our best speaker." The cook nodded. The liquor on her breath was rum. "So warmhearted." She paused, pinching her lips shut, suppressing something that had come up from her belly. "You're just the most warm."

\*

Leaning against the baptismal font at the front of the church in a tuxedo was the cook's cousin, Erik Pederson. He spoke with a dark, plump woman and periodically batted her on her heavy, bare shoulder. When he had done this several times, the woman reached back and whacked him in the chest with the flat of her hand. The sound of the impact was loud. The two of them chortled and tried to conceal their mirth with their hands. It appeared to the cook that his cousin had coerced a woman to marry him; the woman's ring was a salient and gaudy flash in the spare hull of the sanctuary.

The cook lowered his eyes. He would not be caught gazing at the cousin and the wife. However, he was really shocked to see his cousin married. Really shocked.

*

The cook's cousin was an educated man, a scholar of obscure philosophies, an adjunct at some desperate midwestern state university. The man had always been a real bastard. He was about as physically grotesque a person as the cook had ever known. Right below the rim of his belt, for example, the cook's cousin expanded enormously. It had been this way since they were kids. The chest, the shoulders, the back, the stomach—all seemed to have dropped into an expansive bubble of body flesh orbiting the waistline; something, it seemed, had always been herniated. The man's arms were clubby with bloated, hair-thronged fingers that curled into half fists. He suffered from a cleft palate, his lip lifting to his nose and exposing his teeth in a placid grin. Also, an unseemly hunch of the spine.

\*

*When I look out at her family, all of you just sagging there in your pews, dwelling on her life, and now, as it must be, her death, I imagine she would like to have a few things uttered on her behalf. For starters, she might ask that you please stop calling her Mothball.*

\*

The Edens were stopped dead in all eight lanes, both directions. The Pedersons and Leifs were one long snake in the right-hand lane, their headlights turned on in the blazing sunlight, a pathetic gesture. Through the bright windshield of his rental car, the cook gazed at the dogs cluttering the rear window of his cousin's Lincoln ahead. It

was all torsos and heads back there, banging
around, slathering.

\*

The Leifs and the Pedersons were drunk, all of
them, even the children of the children. Blitzed,
they sprawled on the grandmother's living room
furniture laughing about the woman's final days in
her hospital bed, the visits they'd paid her, the
things she'd said in the madness that preceded her
death. Then, one of the Pedersons suggested that
nothing would make the grandmother so proud as
to look down on them and see another Swedish
Castle. The cook immediately produced a wooden
spoon and a paring stiletto like a card trick from his
pants pockets.

\*

There had been no resistance, only brief confusion,
when the cook's cousin insisted on taking the part of
the queen. The cook certainly had nothing to say
about it. None of the boys had ever played the role
of queen before, but if he protested, he would have
had to speak directly to the man and so far he'd
avoided doing so.

\*

She didn't pick up. The cook studied his cell phone for several moments, checking and rechecking he'd dialed the correct number. He had. He dialed again and again received only his own recorded voice. The cook pondered the things she might be doing with their eleven children at this hour. He didn't leave a message.

\*

Of course, there, down the hallway and around the corner, in one of the bedrooms of the grand-mother's house, is the cook's cousin showing the cook a way to peel the skin off a hot dog, a way to suck on certain pieces of candy, a way to play a musical instrument with the lips and cheeks of the mouth. The cook is nine, ten, and eleven there; the cook's cousin fifteen, sixteen, and seventeen.

\*

The queen strode from one side of the living room to the other in a tiara and cape. The monologue was pretty good, obviously prepared: "What must a mother do to her daughters, what must a daughter do to her mothers, her many mothers, to induce harmony like a child in the home?" The queen allowed her question a silent moment, then answered it with a firm fist on the top of the piano. "Harmony must be sired! You cannot wait for harmony. You cannot seduce harmony. You must beget such things." Oh god, he was good, the new Pederson queen; the cook could admit that his cousin was a very good queen indeed.

*

*Still not home, or you're not picking up. I'm worried. Also, I'm obviously sorry I didn't get that flight. Also, I'm drunk. This was harder than I thought. Listen. Look, tell Inger to go to that orientation tomorrow without me; he'll be fine. Have the Ingvilds drive him if he gives you crap. They owe us, anyway. Look, I'm sorry. Everyone here is sad, worse than I can remember.*

*

The cook's cousin left the house to smoke a cigarette and to let his dogs out of the Lincoln to run them. He had three dogs total, it now appeared; the cook watched them from inside the house, through the kitchen window. The grandmother's front yard wasn't large, and it shared a small fenceless lawn with the neighbors on either side. The queen, still in his tiara, threw a blue racquetball for the dogs to charge after. The dogs were large, muscular. They ran after the ball with force, fought and wrangled over the thing like it was raw meat, and then they returned it to the queen's feet with a sort of palsy. They did this numerous times. They were ridiculously oversized compared to their owner, and when the queen picked the ball up and held it above his head, the animals propped their legs on his shoulders and lapped the man's face with their tongues. The cook considered whether the cousin's head might fit inside the mouth of one of the dogs.

*

When the dogs were brought indoors, Per Hans Leif protested. "What if the dogs shit, how will the house be sold?"

"The dogs have already shat," the queen said with coldness. "They'll rest quietly in one of the back bedrooms."

"Then at least put them in Mothball's room—it already smells like shit." All were too drunk to maintain interest in this issue. The queen took the dogs away. The children sat around the coffee table and drew panties on the naked women in Grandfather's nudity magazines, unearthed from the basement.

*

"What I don't understand," the queen's wife protested to the room, "is why I have to be a ghost. I am no ghost. I'm like one of these ladies, you know, who is bigger than the picture. I am no ghost. I have never been some flimsy thing to shake sticks at. Look at me. Look at this!"

*

The cook had a hand at his back. It was the queen's hand, and it slipped around his waist. Before the cook could shift away, he was pulled close to his cousin, so close he could feel a hot, damp armpit wetting his pant leg, the thick ungainly waistline of the queen pressing against his thigh.

"Some group," the queen said. "Some fucking group we got here."

The cook nodded.

"So," the queen said, "I'm going to need you to repeat your eulogy from earlier."

"Why?"

"Because I liked it. It was warmhearted."

The cook said nothing.

"I need warmhearted, Able. You see what I'm doing here as queen. You see that I need some warmheartedness to round out the treachery."

"Maybe you should just scale back on the treachery."

"That's a thought," the queen said. "But do you know what I'm thinking?"

"I don't care about you."

"I'm thinking about how much sweeter you used to be when you were younger."

∗

The cook expected the dogs to be there when he stepped into his grandmother's bedroom. He put his knee through the bedroom doorway first. And, as he expected, he felt a bony face against his knee. He shoved the dog backwards, into the room, closing the door behind.

He went to the bed, sat down. The dogs thrust their faces into his lap. They were happy dogs. He petted them for a short time. The cook listened to his family guffaw and chortle as they sprawled about the grandmother's living room. He could hear the queen through the door requesting a jester to juggle something, wine glasses it would seem, and when the shattering of glass shortly followed, the house quaked with lusty amusement. With his stiletto knife, the cook cut a deep line across one dog's pretty throat. The dying was silent, mostly clean, and without evident suffering. Eyes rolled. The mandible dropped. What stung the cook was the sight of the other two dogs backing away. They studied the dying dog and cowered into the corner, whining softly, or at such a removed and lofty pitch they might have been in another room of the house, perhaps another house altogether.

*

In the third act, the queen had some doubts. These were doubts he claimed he could never utter to his most trusted lords and confidantes, doubts about his decision to disembowel his own parents. "It is trying," the queen contended, "to have to willingly disembowel one's parents."

He weighed his heart as such, feigned torment over his dilemmas, and when the servant entered the stage, the queen wheeled and ordered the immediate death of his parents—he could delay the dirty thing no longer, he barked, lest it burden his conscience further and all of Swedish Castle see his doubts.

The Pedersons nodded, and the Leifs examined the dead grandmother's carpeting. No one was following. The servant, the youngest cousin of the cook, departed without a word to her script, and the queen leaned like a fop on the piano.

\*

*I'm at a loss here. I'm at my wit's end. I'm trying to understand where you are, but I don't even have a guess at this point. Where do you take eleven children in the middle of the night? Anyway, it's almost three o'clock your time. I have done something I shouldn't have. Call.*

\*

Surprising everyone, the king (the cook's older sister) opened the fourth act with a sudden announcement that would, she claimed, "spare the queen his mortal doubts." The king revealed a secret she'd just heard: the princess was illegitimately with child. "Therefore," the king announced, "the princess would be the more fitting substitute for a disemboweling, if in fact the queen felt he could no longer go through with the disemboweling of his own parents." The princess was being played by the servant's newborn, Lily, seven weeks old.

\*

The sobbing was excessive. Upon seeing the butchery in the grandmother's bedroom, the queen stepped outside of himself and wept. He had thrown jewelry and both bedside lamps across the room. One of the dogs had been kicked and injured and had fled beneath the bed; the other was thrown into an adjacent bathroom, locked in there by one of the Pederson men, who had pulled the thing's collar from his son's fist.

It surprised the cook to see this dog's muzzle stained dark with blood; it had evidently stuck its nose into the dead dog. It was the consensus of the room, then, that one of the dogs—maybe both of them—had slain the other. The queen sobbed, He knew it, he knew it, he knew it! He knew this would happen one day!

*

All was silent. The queen's brother, the blacksmith of Swedish Castle, had his socked foot on the dog's smooth, gray pelvis and was moving it thoughtfully, as though trying to rouse it.

*

The queen's air was passing heavily through his teeth. The longer he gazed at the blood-soaked car-peting and the disjointed head of the animal—its teeth exposed along the jowl, its eye open—the heavier his breathing became. The cook had to look away. The queen said he would need just several more moments before he would be able to speak. And when he did speak, finally, he began swearing. The curses did not come clearly through his affected mouth. "Guck," he said.

*

When the queen returned to the living room, he was wearing his tiara and the cape had been restored around his neck, flowing over his shoulders, dragging along the carpet behind his feet. He signaled with a finger to drop the lights.

*

In one final, glorious act, the servant came forward and placed her infant, the princess, down across an ottoman. The queen commanded her to confess the baby's sin, and when she did in the voice of the infant ("I have an illegitimate bun inside me"), the queen carefully placed his cape down on the coffee table, pulled a curtain rod out of his belt loop, and struck the woman—his teenage cousin—with a snap of the rod across the neck. All flinched, then looked to the ottoman, fully expecting the infant to be struck next.

*

*I just hope you're not waiting at the airport. Anyway, this is almost done here.*

*

The queen's father comforted his son with a hand at the back of his neck. "Well," the father said gently. "On the farm you can either shoot them or you can teach them."

*

To teach them, the queen shoved the dog toward the blood pooled in the carpet. He dragged its head toward the severed throat. But smelling the death, the dog resisted and threw its weight backwards; the collar slid up nearly over its ears and would have slipped off entirely if the queen hadn't adjusted and taken the thing by the scruff, thrusting its nose directly into the flaps of skin at the dead dog's throat.

Able watched.

"Bad girl—Bad, ba-aad girl—"

The Pedersons then rolled the big dead dog into a black garbage bag, spun it, and tied the top.

*

It occurs to me that this death is both a crappy surprise for everyone and yet long overdue. When they are among us, those we love are so much among us we pretend we don't need to do anything. And when they are no longer among us, those we love are so much completely gone we pretend we have to do something, everything, to try to bring them back. It occurs to me we probably have this completely backwards.

*

And of course there, down the hall and around the corner, this is the room Able is taken to on private matters with his cousin. There, this is where they skin hotdogs and stick candies in their mouths and, as it turns out in time, thrust each other's penises into the palm of the other's hand until everything is disgusting, cold, and empty.

*

Able looked at the ceiling as the queen spoke about the final act of Swedish Castle. "Don't roll your fucking eyes at me," the queen said. "It's simple. The funeral is the only thing left. A few words by the queen, me, to capitalize on that eulogy—thank you, by the way, real warmhearted—and the cook will be found out to be the father of the illegitimate child of the princess and we'll kill both of them by throwing them alive into an open grave filled with serpents."

The cook rubbed his eyes.

"You're a loose end," the queen explained. "The princess isn't a very good bad guy, being only seven weeks old, et cetera. And neither are you, for that matter, because you just basically stand there with your stupid wooden spoon and do nothing except smirk all night. But the two of you together, and then sealing your grave over, and some heartfelt digressions about love and fidelity by me—that'll be closure."

## PLEASE KEEP SOMETHING
## OUT OF FOUNTAINS

Someone or some group has rubbed or gouged with a sharp or blunt object a critical word from the placard near the fountains. Now no one really knows whom or what to keep out of the fountains. This makes things tricky. It feels very good to fountain. It is very nice to fountain with whatever you want. It is not always nice to fountain with what others want.

So, I hope it's *dogs*.

Dogs fountain regularly. They plunge or charge in like hippopotamuses or typhoons and submerge themselves right beside the babies, the shoes, or the floating empties of gin or beer. For all the fondling or coddling they receive, these dogs often suffer from bad skin irritations or infestations of tiny leaping insects. This blights the fountains like a moral or social illness. Or, perhaps it is *food products*?

This is when Ingrid comes over to discuss the matter. "It's the literal brink of insanity," she says, studying the vandalized placard before us. Ingrid is my daughter and flirts openly with exaggeration. She is very intelligent. She is fifteen. She is my only child. She fountains nude.

"Maybe it is *nakedness*," I say.

"Or maybe it is *institutionalized body bagging*." She is the only person who fountains without clothing. I wear a thong, red cotton. "Anywho," she says, "I blame Hillary totally."

She is not alone. Many fountain angry with the Clintons. The Clintons brought us these fountains back in the late ripping nineties, languaged the rules and regulations on a placard, and then suddenly withdrew just as governance seemed at a critical premium. We have all, at one point or another, written a letter to this effect to one or both of the Clintons. These letters have fallen on deafness or preoccupation, it seems. And were the fountains not so nice, generally speaking, a street campaign in Chappaqua might just be on the docket—

O—*Perversions*! Truly—will the fountaining perversions never stop?

In the meandering canals, the perverts in black sunglasses are ogling my Ingrid from behind, and I must drape a towel over her shoulders. Somehow we have managed to fountain shoulder to shoulder beside these parasites for years without incident. Maybe this was their time. Maybe this was supposed to have been an era without fountain perverts. We may never know now.

But when my Ingrid realizes I've toweled her body, she snaps the towel off and drops or dumps it to the cement. "Don't be crass," she says, and she runs a few steps, stops, turns, and says, "or archaic." Then she runs again, her feet slapping until she leaves the ground full eagle—

I lose my breath. Her golden naked body is suspended along a line that parallels the earth. You wonder in moments like this if this is what the fountains are all about. You wonder as you watch your daughter like this if the difference between having less and having nothing is American humanity.

## TOMTENS

*The tiny creature whose image he saw*
*in the mirror was himself.*
—FROM SELMA LAGERLÖF'S
The Wonderful Adventures of Nils

The boy's father massaged badly: he used only his fingertips and fingernails when stroking his customers. He worked in short, sharp bursts. He pinched. Frequently his fingers would slip, come off the muscle as he was lifting or twisting, and his nails would scrape or gouge a lobe or temple. "God fuck it," he would say. Then he would pause. He would take a long, sound breath. He was a minister. He knew better. The boy would watch his father dab the wounds with cotton balls and return his hands to the body, resume the pinching.

The boy's father had set up his massage chair and station in the front entrance of the local grocery

store. The grocery store had given him the space as
a kindness, for the man was a local minister. Times
were tough. They knew he could use the money.
They couldn't see the harm in having a man of god
with his son posted in the entryway. They knew him
to be a quiet sort of person. They expected he
would remain a quiet person.

Indeed, the boy's father spoke quietly throughout his massages. He talked to every customer.
Primarily, he shared the names of people from his
parish and his professional knowledge of their personal lives. His best lector had credit card debt into
the hundreds of thousands of dollars. He worried
that this man might be stealing from the collection
plate on Sunday mornings. He was unsure if this
man could be trusted. But he was going to give him
a little rope, he would say. The Pedersons, on the
other hand, were more likely stupid than sterile.
They wouldn't make love in the missionary position
because Lena was a control freak and Jorge mil-
quetoast. "I mean I love my parish," the boy would
hear his father say, "but at a certain point physics
and chemistry tell us semen has to stay inside the
woman. You cannot give rope to people like this."

In point of fact, the boy's father seldom had customers. Customers were unexpected. Thousands walked right on by, waving at the minister and his son as they passed. As such, his son was made to fill the hours. The boy really at first had no say in this involvement. He was quite young. His mother had died; his father was plainly alone and poor. When no customers stopped for a massage, and most did not, the father called his son over. If he protested, the boy was seized and dragged and made to put his face into the chair's padded pillow. He held his breath while his father practiced his techniques on him.

The father's techniques were brutal. The man had no training. He had no *touch*. And he seemed to know this. He often asked for his son's feedback. "Stop crying," his father would whisper into his ear, "and tell me how the hell to do this." The one time the boy told him ("Maybe use more palm?"), his father thanked him sharply. The boy was then chopped across the spine in one fantastic blow. Those who were purchasing their groceries at the front of the store heard this. They turned to look at the minister and the boy, facedown in the massage chair. The father smiled at them. He waved. "Tapotement," he explained. "Just the tapotement technique. Very big in China!"

The boy would not offer his feedback again. He stopped speaking to his father. He could be found in the massage chair for six or seven hours a day, listening to his father comment on the lives of people from his church, yet never speaking a word. The father pressed and stroked and pummeled and pinched his son's body. He could feel it give beneath his hands. Whenever the boy's body tried to grow, the father could feel it, so well had he come to know the boy's body, and he pressed and pinched those developments away. As a result, the boy stopped growing. He began, indeed, to shrink. By the age of sixteen, the boy was as big as he'd been at four years old. He required a booster for the massage chair.

Those who walked past the two of them over the years became concerned. They asked the father, sometimes, if he had more than one son. The father only laughed and nodded vaguely. But they were moved. It would have been difficult to ignore: the once-large boy was now a helpless imp. It was clear to everyone what the minister was doing. So they began asking for and offering money for massages, and when they pulled the little boy out of his father's massage chair, they handed him to another person who took the tiny child away to be fed.

They slipped the boy food right from their grocery bags, just out of the sight of the minister. The boy ate frozen fish sticks, chocolate cereal, fruits and vegetables, candy, eggs, tea bags, entire loaves of bread, bags of cornmeal—anything at all they showed him, anything he could grab from their bags. They laughed about it. They were pleased. They did not mind his gluttony. They watched as he snapped up anything he could find. The only thing that stopped him was a can of foie gras.

The boy just looked at it. He smelled the can. He shook it. He looked up at the man who had offered the boy his bag of groceries. The man nodded. "Goose liver," he said. The man took out his pocketknife and cut open the can. He handed it down to the boy. The boy smelled it and fell backwards. His vision blurred. He had to sit up. He swiped his fingers through the foie gras and shoved them in his mouth. He was suddenly in the air. He was out of doors, soaring over the grocery store. He took the wind into his eyes and cried. He yelled out and swept over large spells of forested land, deer herds, and white-tipped lakes. Then he returned to the grocery store. The man was slapping him in the face. "Are you there, little man?" He was shouting. "Are you there?"

The boy went after the foie gras and was flying again. When he returned to the store, he was laughing. He smiled and was red with pleasure. The man laughed and told others to buy the boy goose liver, because it seemed to make him happy. And they did. They shoved it at him. He ate as much goose as they would give him. They shook their heads (What sort of child likes foie gras?), but they brought it to him just the same. And the boy began growing rapidly until his father noticed.

One day the boy was called over. He was told to sit in the chair. The boy situated himself. The father felt the boy's size beneath his hands. "You're a fat Herod," he whispered into his son's ear. "You will be crushed," he said.

"I doubt it," the boy said.

But his father worked against his son's body. He pressed and pinched him. The boy cried out. He squeezed and twisted the boy's flesh. He punched and hacked at it. He pulled a metal bar from the handle of a broken grocery cart and throttled his son's shoulders. But when he returned his hands to the boy's flesh again, he could see that it was not giving way. Still, he went back at the child, punching and kneading and grinding and tearing.

Hearing the boy cry out, an older woman came over and demanded a massage.

"Not now," the father hissed. "I am at work on my son."

"I will pay you well, Pastor," the woman said.

The man paused for just an instant, and the boy slipped from beneath his father's hands. He leapt up and offered the woman the chair.

"Get in that seat," the boy's father said to his son.

But the boy laughed and, though the father lunged to grab him, moved swiftly and sprinted into the depths of the store. There, he was given as much foie gras as the butcher had on hand. He ate it so quickly that it filled his mouth, fell out, and tumbled to the floor. He bent down and licked the floor clean. The butcher shook his head. "I'll order more," he said.

When the boy returned to his father at the front of the store, the massage chair was empty. His father was slumped against it. The boy put his hand on the father's head. His father looked up. "You think you've outdone me," he said. The boy nodded.

His father tried one last time to grab his son, but he had no chance—the boy was too smooth, too quick, and this was the last day of the father's strength, the last day the boy would sit in his father's massage chair.

Each day the father and son returned to the store. They sat and stared at the empty massage chair. They waved or nodded at the people walking past. Often these people greeted the son warmly and asked if he might massage them. The boy's father winced, but he said nothing. The boy would agree. He would ask his father to sit on the stool where he once sat, and he would begin massaging these people. They would pay him well. The boy was quite good. He knew how to touch the body, how not.

This went on for years. The father, slumped and silent, simply watched his son's massaging. Customers would greet the old minister, and he would not reply. They would look at the son, and the boy would smile and shrug. Then one evening, the old minister suddenly fell off the stool. The boy let him lie there until he'd finished his massage. When the customer stood to leave, he asked the boy if he'd like help lifting his father off the floor. The boy thanked the customer, but said he had it under control. When the customer left, the boy went to his father. "Touch me," the father said. "Rub me, please."

The boy said he would not do that, no.

But the father was lying on the tile floor and could not seem to lift himself. He tried to reach for the boy. But the man did not have enough strength. The boy could not ignore it; he was not quite the same person his father had been. He took his father's hand and lifted him to the massage chair. There, he felt his father's body, the shrunken muscle, the thin flesh. The boy tended these gently. He rubbed his father's body with soft supplication, tender rubbing. The father asked him to work harder, push and pinch him.

But the boy would not.

"Hit me," the father begged. "I cannot even feel your hands."

But the boy would not. He would only touch the man more lightly. Sometimes he just let his hands rest on his father's back. He would not move his hands at all, only leave them to rest there on his father's body.

At first this made the father writhe. But in these final days, he began to grow softer and smaller. The boy took no other customers. He carried him from their home to the store, and from the store back to their home. The father breathed shallowly. His final request was something the boy could not hear. When the boy came closer, he asked that the boy speak to him. He asked that the boy shut off the rolling wave soundtrack and tell him what news he'd heard from the church. The boy knew everyone's story at the church, having also taken over for his father there, and yet he withheld.

## WHEN OUR SON, 36, ASKS US FOR WHAT HE CALLS A SMALL LOAN

**D**ays followed the holidays, and I still had meat, wine, and hearth on my teeth. I still wore sweaters. I stroked my crimped, gnarled facial hair. The house was bloated with heat. The porch complained. Windows whined. Family came over on a Sunday night.

My wife approached the dinner table. We were waiting to eat something. Our forks pointed to the ceiling. She announced that she would like, before any of us ate anything, our son to stick a straight edge into her chest. "Up here," she said, pointing to her sternum. "Anywhere in this region." A nearby child was asked for the straight edge. The child had no idea what a straight edge was. "The box cutter," my wife clarified. The child produced the tool from a belt buckle. She handed it to my wife. "O.K.," my wife said, "let's do this."

My son rolled his eyes. He made a dramatic sigh and put his hands on the table. He took a long drink from his small cup of tea. He put this down. He scratched his hair. He rubbed his face. "You see what it's like?" he leaned over and said to his wife. He made large eyes at her. He said to her that he knew they should not have come to this house. He said that she needed to stop making him do things with his own family. He said she should stop bullying him. He raised his finger at his wife.

This child, we love him without condition. He has always been a guru of dramatic force. He has no time for anything. I've never met anyone with less time. He is always "working." Yet we have no idea what he does for a living. When he is not "working" he is in the middle of something abstract: washing something, feeding one of their kids, unplugging something. And he is pointlessly short with us. He will not answer his phone. He will not call us. The circumstances surrounding his life when he *does* finally call are usually so lamentable the first thing you want to say to him is "Good-bye."

The table fell into din. Such is family. My wife told everyone to shut their faces. She looked at my son standing there, drawing back his tea dregs. She sighed. This was hard on her. Love takes a discernible toll.

"Pilate," she said. She tapped her watch. "I have pork loins searing."

My son pushed back from the table. "Fine," he said. He stood. He went over and took the straight edge from his mother's hand. She pulled up her blouse. Someone asked the children to leave. There was some disagreement on this: the children should be included; the children should not be victimized; a family with secrets is a family in hell. It went back and forth. The children wanted to know what the secret was, a fair question. They were told that their aunt, my wife, was to be stabbed in the chest by her son, their uncle. The older children were appalled, and departed; the younger children wanted answers: why would he do this sort of thing? They were told their questions were tedious and they were made to leave.

Then our son approached and stabbed his mother below the breast. She pulled it out. "Try my stomach," she said. He stuck it in her thigh. She winced. She took it out. "You never listen"—and she popped the cutter into our son's ear. I handed his wife a check at the hospital, in the waiting room. It was the right thing to do. I said we were sorry. We were not. My wife fingered the bandage beneath her bra strap. Because she has listened to our son's apologies for years and knows no other sort of apology, his wife doubted our sincerity. She drew their newborn close to her and said something simple.

## WE HAVE THEM TO RAISE US

"This sounds very intellectual," I said to her. "Clearly, this is a game of the mind."

"Yes." She had thought about it a lot during the long days and nights of nursing, she said, and she knew she had to see these men again. She was certain. She needed to see these men again, one more time, as many as would come see her.

I turned a page of the newspaper with tremendous care. I said, "So, this is divorce."

She had just slid a spoonful of cereal into her mouth. She shook her head and made a face. "This has nothing to do with that," she said. I nodded. She chewed. I waited. "Look," she continued, "compared to the time and energy I spent with those guys collectively, you and I just don't have a prayer. No one would."

"You're fascinating."

"Aging is fascinating."

"You just want to say 'hello.'"

"I imagine there's more to it than 'hello.'"

"I'm sleeping in a kitchen chair a lot right now."

"Right?"

I looked up from the paper. She smiled and shook her head while she crunched her cereal. Our child was sleeping in his swinging apparatus upstairs. We were not to let the child sleep in this or any other swinging apparatus, so we were pretending the child was awake.

I went outside, turned on the spigot, and began watering a patch of yellow lawn near the front porch. Days after she'd given birth, she had mentioned a few of her former lovers by name. But I hadn't listened. I wasn't focused on that kind of thing. Things like that didn't matter to me. The new baby had made me unusually thoughtless. I went to the grocery store about five times a day. When she said our son's eyes reminded her of Benjamin, the boy tucked like a football under her arm, nursing, I was running out the door to get kefir and organic fruit. I said, "Yeah," and I locked the door behind me.

The lawn had dried badly. It would not take the water. It pooled as though on cement. After Benjamin, she'd mentioned a few other names too, wistful. Charles came up when it became clear we would need to buy our son a swimsuit for the baby pool—a little infant swimsuit—because Charles used to have the most interesting swimsuits. Charles she would like to see in his swimming trunks again, preferably in Cape Cod, where they had first swum together years ago, when she was nineteen and twenty. And she could also remember him in his navy T-shirt. He had incredible pectorals, Charles, but more importantly he had a way of listening to her talk for hours at a time, a way of making time seem so light and spacious you felt that you'd transcended it. That was Charles, and I'd really not listened. I went back inside.

"I'm worried," I said to her.

"Me too."

"Your worst enemy might be doing this badly. Maybe I could do a magic show for all of you."

She seemed to give this a thought. She looked out the window. Our mutual appreciation of my sense of humor had really degenerated. She said, "I don't know if you'd be here at all, would you?"

"I don't play the oboe," I said.

"I mean, it might be weird to have you two here. I'm not really sure this would be about you or him or us."

"Right," I said. "I understand."

"Do you understand?"

"I understand."

I did not understand. I do not understand.

I was sleeping in the kitchen chair in those days. At night Kimberly would be up handling our screaming son five, six, ten times. I couldn't distinguish the first handling from the last. I didn't know dawn from dusk. I could achieve consciousness instantly, leaping to gather a cloth or a soft thing or an electronic mechanism for her, her voice summoning me from rooms of the house I felt I barely knew, and then I could fall away again in the kitchen chair, uncertain that I'd ever left it, uncertain that I'd ever given her the thing she'd needed. Sometimes she would just materialize across the table from me. I would open my eyes and she would be sitting there across from me. She liked to say, "Are you feeling sorry for yourself?"

Kapler was another early name, Kappy. She had told me, I believe, that our son's flesh smelled the way Kappy smelled after he'd washed himself. This Kappy apparently used to take exceptionally long baths in a large claw-foot tub made of green porcelain, and he'd had the ability to create these enormous suds of soap that went by a name she could no longer remember. To this too I said nothing, nodding, I imagine, as though she'd made a comical remark about my hair. It's astonishing in retrospect. My wife went on to say that, like our son, this man could smell like delicious soap all day. She said she wished she could remember the name of that soap. "God," she said, "I loved that soap." Then she smelled our son deeply and closed her eyes.

Sometimes at work my colleagues drop by my office and say things like, "Can you believe Reynolds is folding?" Or they say, "Can you believe that, in like two months, we'll be eating Turkey, Ohio, with spoons?" I always say "I know" to this sort of positing of the future, because while I cannot believe such things in the present moment, having been burned in the past by things that were not what they'd seemed, I trust that I will entirely believe them after they occur. "I know" is my way of acknowledging that I know how hard it is to believe something that seems likely to happen, but has no god-given assurance of actually happening. If one of these young tycoons had swept into my office and said, "Can you believe your wife is going to ask you to write the invitations asking her lovers to come to your house?" I would have said, "I know," because nothing whatsoever in that period, with a new human having ruptured our lives, nothing in that period would have indicated that she might not, in fact, ask me to write these invitations.

"It's better if you do it," she said. "Less awkward."

"You'd like me to invite your BFs to your BFP."

"Are you sixteen?" Then she explained that she wanted me to write the invitation from her perspective. She said she wanted me to write the invitation in such a way that it *seemed* to be written by her—a direct solicitation—but that if pressed she could say she didn't have "the balls" to write it herself, that "a friend" had written it for her. This would give her the freedom of conscience that she said she needed to be able to look these men in the eye.

"Big Fucking Party," I said. "You're pretty sure they're going to jump at this."

"Oh," she said, "they'll come."

Where was our child during this exchange?

I told her then that I would be really touched to have the opportunity to drum up the invites, but I mostly wondered if maybe she didn't simply want to sleep with other men, if this weren't all one unnecessarily elaborate ruse, if perhaps she felt she needed to go to these lengths to more gently convince me she wanted out of our marriage. I have never been good sexually, and it would not have shocked me to hear her say it. I have a prodigious sense of humor, but I am woeful in sex, I have long known, and certainly I would have been keen on the matter right at that time, right in that stretch following the birth of the child, when the thing that most defined me were the consequences of sex. For her to go to these lengths—it all seemed so unseemly, so executive and corporate. And yet I didn't blame her. I'm not great with giving pleasure or blame to others. It's all too direct.

She handed me the empty electric bill envelope sleeve with a list of thirty-six names enumerated on the back—enumerated. I could not be certain if they'd been numbered in terms of chronology or importance. There were names on that list I hadn't heard of; there were several names I knew well and was surprised to see included.

"I thought Travis was just your brother's friend," I said to her.

She gave our son her breast. "Please don't judge me," she said. "Most women my age have lists that could roll out the door."

"Thirty-six?"

She tipped her head to her shoulder. "Don't judge me."

"What do you want with Travis?"

She blew on our son's hair.

"Maybe," I said, "we should bring in my old girl-friends, really break this thing wide open."

She laughed. She really started laughing. It was the first time I'd heard her laugh like this since the baby was born. She had a wonderful laugh, and when she really laughed an honest and vulnerable ghost of our pasts emerged. But then the laughter angered our son, and he pulled away from her breast and wailed. That was that. My wife swore at the child and left the room with him.

I had at that point never created an electronic invitation. I have since that time done many, many electronic invitations. I have become quite capable with that technology. I remember that in my first run, the creation of the invitation was neither difficult nor easy, neither pleasing nor horrible. I remember it was more satisfying, when it was all completed, than I'd expected. The primary image of the electronic invitation, which pleased me above all else, bore a clip-art image of businessmen and one businesswoman collaborating on a project in an office cubicle. The woman was sitting behind the computer, her hand on the mouse, with a team of suited men hunkering all around her, behind her, gazing at her work on the screen. One man had his hand on her shoulder. They were all huddled very close. Most were smiling as though a joke had just been told. One or two looked very, very serious: they were not at all amused to be working on this project: "You're invited to come to my home to see me again—Kimberly!"

Kimberly and I were introduced by friends at a small and overwrought party on the north side of

Chicago. At that point we were in our late twenties. Like most graduates of Northwestern, we started our uninspired careers in some approximation of a low-tier business position. We were both living in gritty neighborhoods on the north side. We both thought dogs were funny. We both seemed harmless enough to one another—not particularly cool, or not cool enough to be threatening, and not painfully annoying. We were both interested in being financially solvent without being obsessed or controlling about money, and that was sexy enough to get us started. I asked her on a date to a Cubs game. I hated baseball; so did she. We laughed about it. We left after the second inning. We got tipsy at a bar. We went to her place and slept together. We dated a few more times. Families were met. I proposed. She accepted. We had lame careers in promising full swing. We bought a new condo together with towering metal cabinets in the kitchen and a ceiling as high as the building itself. We waited a few years to have a baby and said to people regularly that we were waiting to have the baby until after we'd lived, having no idea whatsoever what this meant. We traveled once out of the country, to London, and we felt that was enough travel for the rest of our lives. We made a baby. It took a lot of sex. It took a lot of UTIs. We waited and she worked with me on the sex. It happened: the baby came.

Of course I entertained violent acts. I am only human. I am subject to human pain, and I am subject to human helpless rage in the face of human pain. I did not carry the violent acts much further than picturing myself buying a gun and carrying it home to a house full of nude men who were lounging about with long-stemmed goblets of wine in their fists. This violent moment usually culminated in me just sort of standing there in the doorway with my handgun, staring at them having sex with my wife behind flimsy sheer curtains.

But, passivity is not about *doing nothing*. It has nothing to do with the absence of action. Passivity has nothing to do with *allowing things to happen*. It simply means you subordinate, make less prominent the agency of action. A great deal can be accomplished in passivity. Take the sudden and inexplicable presence of the e-mail addresses of all thirty-six men, for example. Who knows how these arrived in my electronic invitation? Who knows when or by what means my wife dropped these into the invitation I was to send. Suddenly, they were just *there* and my job was basically already done for me.

Or, take my plans to sabotage and humiliate my wife, myself, my family, and my life, in response to my wife's needs. I'm not sure at all how that sabotage came about, but there were the plans, unfurling.

She had been clear about my role: I was to have no salient role. "Let's just keep it simple." She'd said simpler was easier. "Guys," she said, "like simple."

Within two hours of my having sent the invitations, seventeen of thirty-six responses had been returned. They were interested. One of them responded with the "Hell Yee-ah!" button. The washing machine was on. Someone had poured me a glass of juice, or someone had put it in my hand. Men on the West Coast were replying to my wife's invitation at two in the morning their time. They wrote additional notes to her like "Kick Your Ass Soon!" and "You Rocking!" and "Can't wait babes!" Somewhere my son was screaming at my wife. A man named Kit wrote in his message that "Strange is for people who do not know anything other than their own lives." He too used the "Hell Yee-ah!" button.

"I just can't believe," she said at some point around dawn, "how much these guys want to see me."

"You're a fascinating person," I said.

She began exercising. She gave me the child and a bottle of formula, and said, "Go time."

I looked down at my son and plugged his unhappy little mouth. "Everything's new," I said.

She started a video in the living room that promised to shred her. She was shredded by a militant dark-haired woman in almost no clothing for forty-five minutes. The boy fell asleep in my arms while we were watching his mother move rapidly, in harsh and hostile motions. I flinched whenever she had to thrust. The boy was rapt until he slept. The woman shredding my wife, she was just terrifying.

Then my wife went outside and ran down the street. I quickly put the sleeping child in a stroller and tried to keep up with her, but she was running so fast and so far I couldn't, after a while, see her in the distance. I just kept walking. After several miles, I returned the way I'd come, expecting to find her there at home, perhaps in the shower. But she wasn't there, and she didn't appear until she hobbled into the kitchen almost two hours later. She said, winded, "Fuck." She had her hands on her hips. She was slick and foul. She tore her clothes off and went upstairs, where she would fall asleep on the bathroom floor, the shower running. I found her there.

All thirty-six invitations had been Received within twenty-eight hours. No one had pushed the "So Sorry" button. One wrote to communicate that he "Can't Say Fo Sho." They were all very excited, very spirited, and very capable of dropping everything in their middle-aged personal and professional lives to see my wife. My wife was very flattered by it all. I discovered her in the middle of a regrettable conversation with her sister one afternoon. She said, "I doubt he remembers *that*." Then she was silent as her sister spoke. Then she laughed in a way that seemed, frankly, a little hurtful.

But the earliest construction of sabotage took shape in half-consciousness at our kitchen table in the middle of the night. Our son was screaming upstairs. A woman approached me. She had three men flanking her. She was dressed in a barista's smock. The men wore burlap coffee sacks. She winked at me and said, "How do, Simple?"

I winked back at her and said, "I like it simple."

That's when I came to, my wife at the table staring at me, midsentence. "Did you hear anything I just said to you?"

"Yes." I rubbed my face. She nodded. It became obvious how to ruin her expressed needs.

Good old Jamie wrote, "I cannot wait to hold you again." He was the single "Can't Say Fo Sho" and had now switched to a "Hell Yee-ah!"

I remembered Jamie. Kimberly had told me several times before the baby about Jamie, and that Jamie was the best kisser she'd ever dated. She'd said that, for all his problems, and she never said what those problems might have been, for all his problems Jamie always knew how to kiss. And she used to tell me that Jamie had told *her* that she kissed very nicely too, and because she had kissed a great many people in her life, had experienced some of the worst kissing any human had ever experienced, she knew what good kissing was, and when a good kisser compliments you, you know you're getting high praise.

This was a tricky one, because I didn't exactly think Kimberly was a great kisser. She had a dry mouth and a small, coarse tongue that always felt, I thought, too insistent. My wife had many outstanding qualities; kissing wasn't on the top of that list. I imagined that either Jamie was lying to take advantage of my wife when she was younger, or he was in fact not that great at kissing at all, which would probably mean that she liked Jamie for reasons unrelated to kissing and either couldn't accept this or wasn't fully aware of it, or was fully aware of her expansive interest in Jamie and needed, somehow, to express it indirectly to the man she had actually chosen to marry.

Thirty-six men were coming to my house to see my wife, because she had asked. She had simply asked if thirty-six men would like to fly from around the country to celebrate her thirty-first birthday, and thirty-six men said they would like to do so. "A great many men like your mommy," I said to our son. I was trying to make the child belch but not vomit. I had him pitched over my shoulder, and I could feel the burning in my legs as I bobbed up and down. I tried to make a little song out of it, trying over and over again to think of the word that rhymed with "mommy."

I was alone with our son more often, and he became increasingly unhappy with my company. He was developing mistrust. The mother would hand him to the father, and the father would never hand him back. My son did not like that. His dislike intensified. He stopped falling asleep while eating. He would drink the entire bottle I offered him, top to bottom, just suck the hell out of that thing in long, angry drags, and instead of closing his eyes, he would become increasingly alert as he drank, increasingly anxious and angry, and when that bottle was emptied he would burst into a scarlet song that could devastate windowpanes.

And sometimes Kimberly would just walk past the two of us like this, and the child would smell her and immediately stop his singing. He would whimper, and the whimper would precipitate well-documented physiological realities that Kimberly had hoped to shred, she'd said, and she would flee the room then, and the child would begin singing again, and it came to a point, about mid-July, where Kimberly would ask me where I planned to be with the child and for how long, so that she could plot her life around this.

Airplane tickets had been purchased and electronically expressed to each boyfriend, after not just a few hundred hours of e-mails and communiqués securing necessary travel information from the strange men on the other end of the wires. Hotel reservations had been made. Dietary requests had been received, processed, and forwarded. I felt extraordinarily grateful that the limousine company had thrown in a fourth vehicle without charge for the weekend. In total, preliminary estimates seemed to point toward a weekend costing just under one hundred thousand dollars. I slid these figures across the table to Kimberly, who studied them and said, "But when you consider how much we're getting, though."

Someone at my office had suggested I might put in for a better-paying position that had just opened up. I hadn't really considered needing more money until that time. The sabotage would double the cost of the arrangements, and I wondered how people who didn't have money managed to hold together a marriage with children. I wondered what someone like, I didn't know, a teacher did with marriage. Being married was expensive. It perplexed me for a while, before I fell asleep, how the rest of the world could afford to stay married.

The sabotage of course required a destination, a simulacrum of ours, and I found a nice five-bedroom rental outside Madison without too much difficulty. My coworkers loved the idea of a party so much they willingly and eagerly dolled it all up, helped pull the catering, drinks, and music together. When it comes to parties, young singles don't ask many questions. Not many single people worry about the logistics of planned social events. The men from my office would blend in with my wife's lovers. My specific roots are northern Midwest, settlers near Green Bay, and while we know our way around the labyrinth of deception, because we are half the time misleading ourselves, we are not actually well prepared genetically for the confined chambers of overt and sustained lying. We don't have the energy for it. Yet, this all came together so seamlessly, so naturally, it took the breath away.

Ten days out, I took on some troubleshooting from work:

Kit could purchase sandals in a store not far from the house, yes.

Matthew could be driven to see his great aunt in a relatively nearby city, yes.

Patrick and Steven T. would not find the humidity terribly high at night.

Link could not *expect* to have oral sex again while high on cocaine, no, but Kimberly really missed those days too, and only in the stark contrast of her present life can she take pleasure in what was, for her, a very difficult emotional time.

David had to realize that he was not the only man being invited to the event, and could not therefore expect to take one of his "special drives" again.

Benjamin had a great memory, and he was welcome to bring photographs, of course, but Kimberly did not actually remember the time they had fallen asleep in the hotel sauna in Gainesville, was he sure it was *her*?

It did not seem likely that Kimberly would be able to have a private dinner with Ken, Rick, or Steven L.

Christopher should be grateful he had a wife and family, and there was no need to denigrate them in writing (or in speech), and he should keep his personal shit private or else he would find himself disinvited.

No, Dick, Kimberly did not hang on to that sweatshirt of his, she doesn't think, but she could buy him another one on eBay if he wants. She is sorry about that.

Some of the basic ground rules permitted that I could answer in the affirmative if I were asked if I was her husband and the child's father—she said she could not bear the thought of me having to lie about this—but I was not permitted to bring the matter up with any of the guests. And, generally speaking, I was discouraged from being around at all. I was to remain in the bedrooms upstairs throughout the scheduled events. I was not to feel that I *had* to remain upstairs—she said she could not bear the thought of me feeling as though the child and I were being imprisoned in our own home, locked in some attic like mental invalids from literature—but Kimberly had been clear that I should feel as though it would be best for her if I were to minimize my interaction with the events. If I did come downstairs, with or without the child, I would be encouraged, she said, to not overdo the *protective husband* thing. Don't say things like, "We've been happily married for, et cetera, et cetera." That's annoying. "Don't spoil this for me." And I was not to let them gaze at the child. "Keep the child out of sight as much as possible," she said. She had typed up and printed many of these considerations, and number fifteen was phrased, "Do not go out of your way to stress my relationship to either of you."

I took the e-mail addresses from the women who responded to the paper-plate tags I posted in the grocery store. Seventeen females and three males responded. I created another electronic invitation, this one with a clip-art image of a girl dancing in a shower of ticker tape, and invited them for interviews at the Madison simulacrum. They each arrived on time, and they each interviewed for twenty minutes. I took down information with pen and paper. I told them everything about the evening. I told them what the expectations were, and what they were not. I told them that they should only think about this as a chance to meet some new guys, pretending to have known them without really stressing that knowledge. "It's been, in some cases, fifteen years," I pointed out, "so you can basically just keep saying, 'I have no idea,' and go from there."

Not one of them flinched. I felt a cinder block in my stomach and imagined my knuckles coursing against a sidewalk throughout these interviews, but not one of my candidates flinched at the prospect of openly lying to deceive the wife of a complete stranger. It all seemed entirely appropriate to them. It all seemed like something they'd done before, something they would likely have to do again. And in the end, the woman I chose was the woman who said to me, "Look, I've been married for eight years, and I'm just looking to bring a few options back onto the table for myself."

"You understand thirty-six men will be in the room for the specific purpose of talking at you."

"I understand that, yes."

"Do you want to know why we're doing this?"

She laughed. "Your brain is worth eight thousand dollars cash, and mine isn't."

The night before the men were to arrive, Kimberly tried on dresses. It was nearing ten o'clock. She was spinning and turning, looking at herself in the full-length mirror. She had lost the weight she'd gained from the pregnancy, and more, actually, though she didn't think so. She kept pressing on her stomach. She was saying she hoped this was a good idea, but I watched her and openly doubted that she was seriously questioning her event.

"Hormones hatch some crazy shit."

"I could cancel this thing in an instant." I snapped my fingers.

Kimberly just turned from side to side and looked over her shoulder in the mirror. She didn't say anything. And I didn't continue asking. Our child sucked on her bra straps on the floor.

The men were varied, mostly dark haired. They struck me as older than I'd expected. They appeared to have aged much, much worse than I had. When they approached me at the airport (I had a sign I was holding outside of Security), I asked the more attractive and assertive ones how they were doing. I couldn't help myself. I had been told not to speak with them at all. But I felt it would have been irresponsible to have followed this advice. Part of me thought my wife, deep down, would have wanted me to do this against her expressed will.

I asked James, a tall man in sandals, from Des Moines, if he was looking forward to the weekend. James said he wasn't sure. He said he found the whole thing *surreal*. "It kind of blows my mind," he said. When he received the invitation his first thought was, apparently, "Yes, absolutely," and it was only after he'd accepted the invitation that he realized how odd it was. "She's probably married and divorced," James said. "I hate divorced women."

"Seems like you have a lot you want to share," I said.

James slapped me on the back.

I piled him into the limousine with about a third of the other men. I told them to have a few drinks, compliments of the lady, and that they could freshen up at the hotel before they were taken to the house.

I thought my wife looked younger, standing there in the stunning disaster that had been her plans. The caterers were whispering. I'd called her several times over the course of several hours to let her know that no one had come through the security checkpoints. I had by then dropped off most of the men at their hotel and driven back to our home. The musicians were rehearsing and then sitting silently, looking at their strings. A handyman we'd hired quietly fiddled with the hanging lanterns. Kimberly just stared off. She had read the e-mails I sent to the men. "But how could no one have seen your sign?" she wanted to know. "Is it really possible they would all simply take advantage of the free airfare and ignore the signs?"

"They'll call."

She looked at me. I knew she knew something was amiss. I didn't care. I told her I would go back to the airport. She seemed to know something was wrong, but she seemed grateful to at least hope that she knew nothing. I did not understand. I could not understand. So I left under the ruse of the airport and followed the sabotage.

I remember that at first I felt I needed someone who *looked* like my wife to pull this off. My wife has a sort of fair-haired Swiss Miss Danish princess look, and I found it excruciating to approach women with an eye toward their physical similarities to my wife. The woman I ultimately chose *was* blonde, but she did not look at all like my wife, not really, not now and not in the years she would have known quite a few of these men. I remember hoping the men had forgotten what she looked like. I really bit my nails about this. But I don't know what I was thinking. I could have brought in a Hungarian farmer from the eighteenth century.

Twenty-nine men fill a room in an unpleasant way, I discovered on that Friday evening, and the remaining seven men, who trickled in later, made it even worse. The idea that I should leave my wife alone among this hot throng struck me as impossibly naïve. Most of the men seemed uneasy but eager. The woman I'd hired to be my wife seemed not at all affected. She was speaking with a small group and laughing, and touching their shoulders, touching her hair. She was introducing them to one another. She was talking about what they'd done together, when, where, and the extent to which it pleased or horrified her. She was somehow very natural at this, and it occurred to me that what I'd asked her to do was not really that different from courtship, where most of what you communicate are heavily sutured falsehoods.

Most of the men were more than pleased to help her where she made mistakes in their histories. Most of the men seemed to know immediately this woman was not Kimberly, my wife. But if they did know, they didn't care, or they were willing to overlook it. They drank heavily, and they ate everything they could eat. They swam in the rented pool. They began making phone calls. They played with my son's fingers and they surprised him with peek-a-boo. They shook hands with my coworkers, and they chased after other women and men I'd invited from the office.

I tried to see my wife in this context. I tried to see her touching her hair and touching the shoulders of these men. I tried to ask my son if he liked seeing Mommy having so much fun like this, and he cried.

I approached my proxy wife and interrupted her conversation with Link and Jess and David M. She looked at me suspiciously. She looked worried. She tried to take the hands of my son, who was pinned to my chest in the Björn, but I turned to my side. I said, "Hi."

She smiled and tried to turn back to the guys who were, in odd manners of masculinity, reaching to shake my hand and introduce themselves to me. I kept my eyes on her, however. I thanked her. "This," I said. "This was a really special idea."

She nodded.

The guys around us agreed, though they looked at one another then, with some strangeness. I apologized for interrupting them, and I asked what they'd been discussing. They seemed not to know. So I said, "What's it like seeing all your boyfriends again?"

"It's better than planned," she answered.

"I remember," I said, "when I first started dating you."

She just looked at me, shifting back on her hip and taking a sip of her drink. She seemed to concede that she had not known who I was or what I would be capable of.

I put my hand on her shoulder. I looked her squarely in the eyes. She had delightful, lively eyes. She looked, in a way, frantic. In another way, she looked exhausted. "I feel," I said, "like I don't know you. I feel like, standing here looking at you, maybe I've never known you."

Some of my coworkers were looking at me. They'd met my wife. They tried to conceal their fascination. They thought, surely, that no one could remain what they'd always been. People change, they surely thought. Surely they thought, How bizarre, monogamy. And as though I somehow stood at the foot of all things reliable in their lives, surely they thought, What the hell comes next?

"Well," she said, "we were never as close as you thought we were."

The men liked this. They whistled and rallied behind her. I laughed. She was a good sport. I said that her trampishness was so complete I doubted very much if there was a man in the room who could say he didn't feel as though she knew him better than he knew her.

She nodded. "Last time I checked," she said, "that's the way men prefer it."

"Are you married?" I asked her.

She shrugged.

The men cheered. I noticed Steven T. was growing anxious. He had something he wanted to say.

"Listen," I said to her. "Let's go. Let's get out of here. Let's leave this B-squad here to give one another handjobs, and let's just stop pretending."

She looked confused. She considered it. I felt it then, and I feel it now. She really gave it some sincere thought. I don't know what she would have done with me had she left. But Steven T. didn't like it. He had heard enough, and he came between us, and he looked in my face. "Take that fucking baby out of here," he said.

I laughed. My son had fallen asleep. I went in to give my strange employ a kiss, and Steven T. pushed me away from her. The room bristled. My coworkers started moving in toward me and Steven T. There was some pushing. I stood my ground. "Kimberly," I said. "Come on. Come with me. These guys are not for you."

She nodded, and she looked right in my eyes. My fake wife gave us long, deep consideration. She made a big show of her teeth. She turned, and I walked home to my real wife with my son's head lolling in slumber before me.

In her view of the event, I imagine, my Kimberly stood before these men and made them at ease, the way she had done when they had been younger and *together* in various ways. She was an easy person with whom to talk and be. She was not overly proud of her intelligence, and her intelligence was not so impressive that she suffered from self-awareness. She listened relatively well, and she was very funny. She was incredibly, strangely sharp at games, board games and social/interactive games that involved guesswork and feeding people suggestions toward a specific answer. In her mind, I imagine, she wanted to experience the rush that is putting people at ease, of making them comfortable enough to be reasonable. She had lost this, she felt, and she desperately wanted it restored. She could do a *job*. She could run a marathon. She could keep a budget and make more or less anything she needed to make with her bare hands. She could nurse a child. She could be married. She could make a clown good at sex. But she could not be who she had been, and that upset her, and she told me someday I would understand. But I did not understand. I do not understand so much, and I did feel sorry for myself when she contacted a few of the men directly in the months that followed, and the pieces of the sabotage fell into obvious place. It looked as clunky to her then as it looks to me now, and it feels as childish to me now as it did to her then.

I tried to speak to her directly about all of it, but when I looked into her eyes, I found myself looking into a mirror with about thirty-six strange faces looking back at me. She studied me as one studies a fraction, and she asked me to please accept her need to end our marriage. We split our son down the middle. She wanted half, and she wanted me to have the other half. I look at him now, at the half that I have chosen, and I want to give it back to the rest of him, still having no understanding of how a person is built.

# CABINS

## 1.

**P**resuming he was still well married, I told one of my friends I could not imagine living near my wife in divorce. I've always imagined experiencing my divorce alone in the wilderness, I continued. I have a cabin. I have a boat. I can see my little cabin from where I sit in the boat. The water is slapping the boat. I'm on an elevated chair whipping lures that race across the surface of the water as I reel them back in. My wife is not nearby. In my cabin, as in my entire life in divorce, she's not anywhere to be found or heard or smelled.

And I miss her. I am morose and broken without her in my cabin. If I cannot have her, I can have no one and no thing except my cabin and my boat. The idea of having her part-time, it's unthinkable. It is the galling grotesque of sitcom television. I can't think about it. I walk and drink a lot. Sometimes I walk drunk down the road to the bar just to get more drunk. Sometimes the local girls at the bar hit on me, but I've been there long enough, rejected their advances so often and so sadly, they mostly just stand at the bar and call me by the name they've made up for me, Deer Eyes, and they feel for me as one tends to feel for roadkill. I stumble back to my cabin drunk. I cry, I sleep, I fish, and I live off money I could not possibly possess. "I'm sorry," I said to my friend, "I'm just making this shit up."

## 2.

A different friend had called me shortly before this and invited me to a side of town I'd never considered visiting. That night, cruising in the right lane, I spotted through the passenger window the address he'd given me: it was a hookah bar. I pulled over and went inside. He was sitting in a booth by himself. I slid across from him. "I have news," he said.

"You're dying," I said.

"A little," he said.

"This is a nice place," I said.

He looked around the room. He said, "Yeah, man." Then he said that going to places like this was part of his new life philosophy. He put a black rubber hose in his mouth. He inhaled, I waited, he coughed. He handed me the hose. I just held it. I looked around while he cleared his lungs. I had not seen so many young people in the same room since college. I felt very old, very ridiculous holding my hose. I gave it back to my friend. He said he was divorcing. Then he put the hose in his mouth again and closed his eyes.

I fought the urge to call my wife. I had my hand on my phone. Instead, I got up and ordered a festive piece of cake. My wife and I had talked about these two a lot. They were not a pleasant couple to be friends with. We desired to be rid of them. They seemed to love each other in a way that made us nauseous. He always told her what to do; she always told him to fuck himself. And then they would laugh. We assumed they'd be together forever like this.

I returned to the table and watched my cake ooze lard. My friend detailed his wife's affair, or

what he called "the pin that popped their balloon."
His wife had apparently known this other man for
decades. They were friends in grade school. They
had not spoken in years and then, for reasons that
no one but god could understand, they *ran into
their souls* at a nearby car dealership on a Saturday
evening. After decades of being married to other
people, my friend told me, his wife and this guy
bumped into each other while shopping for cars
and, just like that, *ran into their souls*.

"Not their *soul mates*," he clarified. "Their
*souls*."

"Ah," I said.

"Anyway," he added, pulling his mouth away
from the hose just as he'd brought it to his lips, "You
just hope for this kind of thing for everyone." Then
he inhaled, released, and coughed.

I said, "O.K."

He went on to explain that his wife and her new
man had each thought of one another over the
years, apparently many times. They did not realize
they'd lived in the same city all of this time.
"Apparently," my friend said, straight-faced, "The
guy made a birthday cake for her every year to

commemorate her birthday—then he'd go and dump it in a fire pit in his garden and burn it."

"What about your daughters?" I asked.

"My folks are divorced," he answered.

I nodded. "So, you've told them about all this."

"They know."

I nodded.

He took another long drag from his hose and looked up at me. "Single parent," he said, short of air. "There's a lot of street cred in that these days."

"You're kind of blowing my mind right now," I said.

He exhaled. "Yeah," he said. He didn't cough. He began studying the hookah, as if he hadn't realized this huge futuristic tower had been there between us the whole time. "Well," he said, "I basically just want to kill myself."

## 3.

I took him to my car. I acted cool. I called my car a name. He laughed. He seemed fine. In the car, however, as I drove through his neighborhood, he began knocking his head against the passenger window. I studied him from my periphery. I began talking about my heart attack the previous fall. He said he had heard about it. He was sorry. He wasn't interested, but it seemed right to continue talking about myself. I believed I was offering us both some greater context for our rather narrow sorrow. I told him in detail what I could remember about the catheter. When I pulled up to his house, I extended my hand. "Thanks," I said.

He didn't move. He didn't take my hand. He just stared straight ahead.

"You still living together?"

He nodded.

"That hurts," I said.

"You would think so," he said. Then he invited me in. He said he had some beer in the fridge.

I said I needed to call my wife first.

He clicked his teeth. "Ah," he said. He wagged his finger in my face.

"I know," I said, "I know." I forced a light laugh. I looked at my phone.

He didn't move.

"I'll be up there in just a minute," I said. "You can leave the door open."

"I don't want to be left in that house alone with her anymore."

I dialed my wife. She didn't pick up. The machine came through. I left a vague message about being *on my way* and withheld any expression of love I might have shared were there not a divorced friend sitting beside me.

We walked up to his house and went inside. It was dark. "I can't see anything," I said.

"She's in here somewhere," he said.

### 4.

In bed the night I made the remarks on my divorce cabin, I rolled over to look at my wife. She was reading a book on the history of crochet and needlework. I said, "If we divorce, who gets the baby?"

### 5.

The next morning, I played basketball with a third friend I'd presumed married. I told him about my recently discovered divorced friends. I told him I couldn't understand people divorcing. "It seems," I said, "like an incredible amount of work." Then I shot a layup.

My friend was silent, until he told me he'd always believed marriage was for the brainwashed dickheads of a Hallmark psychological takeover. I passed him the ball and said, "I think Maya Angelou's cards are actually pretty cool."

"That's because you're gay," he said.

I tried to be cool about this. He hadn't gone to school, this particular friend. I had always thought him to be a rough but decent sort—a simple man with values and priorities that approximated my own. But I didn't really know this to be true. I said, "Aren't we all?"

He drained a left-hander from the short corner and looked at me. He shook his head. "No," he said.

"I bet your wife loves your marriage," I said.

"Not unless she's fucking it," he said. Then he said, "We tanked it last year."

"No way," I said.

He was dribbling the ball between his legs. "I was like Helen Keller on drugs in that marriage. I beat the shit out of everything in that house. That marriage was costing us both a fortune. I broke like ten thousand dollars in walls."

He drove the lane. I did not contest this. He rolled the ball over the rim. I'd met this guy about the time of my heart attack at that same gym. The first time we'd shot together, he brought beer to the court and made me try to finish the case with him. We might have pulled it off, had he not broken his leg trying to grab a rebound before it went into the small set of aluminum bleachers near the emergency exits. I had to drive him to the hospital. Both of us were drunk, and I became more drunk as I sat there in the waiting room with his wife, a cool woman. I talked to her for a long time while her husband was in surgery. Then I fell asleep. When I woke up, she was gone. I was just sitting alone in the hospital lobby. I thought she had perhaps gone off for coffee. I sat there for two hours. I checked the nurse's station. My friend had already checked out.

I shot from about six feet. The ball hit the rim and came right back to me. I shot again. "What do you do now?" I asked. "Are you dating?"

He told me he was doing my mother. He snapped the ball off the glass and ran the length of the court.

He ran back. He stood in front of me. He told me to take that look off my face. He told me I made him sick. Marriage, he said, made him sick. Then he walked off the court, taking the ball with him.

## 6.

It's a good cabin. I think about it a lot. I go there a lot. The walls are wood planks. I collect these planks from the back of the mill, where they dump the rejected wood. I throw the planks in the back of my old truck. The truck has no muffler. I drive the planks back to the plot of land I've bought from the state. With a hammer and saw, I build the planks into walls. I make my cabin. It takes me a summer and fall. I sleep on dirt until I'm finished. I eat berries. I eat the perch I can catch from the shoreline. In the first winter after the divorce, the average temperature is ten degrees. I drink a lot. I work on insulating the walls of the cabin and drink. I sometimes walk into town drunk and go to the bar to become more drunk. I talk to no one. I think only of my wife, and when I do talk to someone I talk only of her. I say she is the love of my life. I say she means more to me than living. I am told I need to shower. I am told I need to have my cheeks looked at. I am told my nose is turning black from frostbite. One night a man approaches me at the bar. He says he would like me to look after myself. He tells me I have a lot of people worried about me. "You have good friends," he says. "You have a life," he says. "You're an important person in the world, no matter who your wife may be." He tells me I have a choice: I can move forward with my life or I can sit here in a bar in no-man's-land and lament one broad in a million. I stand up. "My wife is my life," I say.

That's all I remember because I pass out. When I wake up, I am in my cabin. A beautiful Nordic lady is washing the kitchen counter with a white cloth. The room is glowing with soft light. She has made a fire in a fireplace I have no memory of building into the planked walls. She has decorated the cabin with lovely red and blue fabrics and floral tapestries. She has an apron on. She has a scarf on her head. She brings me a mug of hot cocoa. She says she is the Swiss Miss girl all grown up and has come from the hills to take care of me and become

THE RISE & FALL OF THE SCANDAMERICAN DOMESTIC

my wife. She is in love with me. She knows this is sudden. She says, "Oh, Deer Eyes!" But I stop her. I tell her I am sorry. I am. I'm already married.

## 7.

The fourth well-married friend I discovered divorced was my former neighbor. He was driving by his old house, as he often did, and he'd seen me weeding in my front yard and pulled over. He rolled down his window. He told me he was on his way to the state penitentiary. He told me he had started a therapy group for inmates who were, had been, or feared they would soon likely be divorced from their partners and spouses. He said, "You should come."

I went over to his car. I laughed. I said, "You're the fourth person to talk to me about divorce in the past few days. What's up with that?"

"You should come with me," he said.

"Why would I do that?" I asked.

"Empathy," he said.

My friend is not a therapist. He is a dog surgeon with a specialty in genetic eye disease. He and his wife were our neighbors for several years. They divorced just before they moved out. They were extraordinarily public about their divorce. They fought brutally in their home with the windows open, and they made love brutally in their home with the windows open. Even the discrete neighbors in the area talked about them. They often shouted the word *divorce* at one another. You could hear that word on the wind so often it became a sort of third person in their arguments and lovemaking sessions.

"Listen," I said. "When did you guys know it was time to get divorced?"

"When we first got married," he answered.

## 8.

That night, I tell my wife about all my friends who are suddenly divorcing. I tell her about our former neighbors and my afternoon at the state penitentiary. I tell her about the dude at the gym. I have my head in her lap. I look up at her, and she is sleeping.

She is very pregnant. She is deep into our pregnancy. She is sleeping even when she is not asleep.

I keep talking. I tell her about the first guy to tell me he was soon to be divorcing, and how he was still living with his wife. I tell her that the first thing I wanted to do, when he told me this, was to tell her. I tell her that I didn't know, at first, what to say to a person in his position. I tell her that I didn't realize so many people were divorcing in the world. I tell her I do not know what I would do if we divorced.

I let these remarks flitter away into the silence of our living room, and I look up again at my wife. She is a pretty sleeper. "Anyway," I say, "I tried to call you. You didn't pick up. So I went with him into his house. He asked me to follow him into the kitchen to get a beer. And I did. I asked him if I should take my shoes off. He laughed. I asked if we should turn on the lights. We went into the kitchen and stood across from each other at his center island. We kept the lights off. The moonlight from outside lit his face. He just stared at me, or he seemed to be. 'You all right?' I asked.

"'Sad,' he said.

"Then he turned around, flung open the refrigerator, and wrenched a beer open with his hands. He drank back on it and then slid it over to me. I

looked at it. He said, 'You want one of your own?'
He went back to the fridge, pulled out another
beer, palmed the bottle, and almost started to open
it for me, but then he stopped and stood stock still.

"I said, 'What?'

"He whispered, 'Listen.'

"I said, 'I hear the house fan.'

"'I hear her breathing,' he said.

"I said, 'O.K.'

"'I hear her breath,' he said.

"Then I heard something too. I heard footfalls
on the staircase. It was quiet at first, then his daughters pattered into the kitchen. It became suddenly
very noisy. We flung on a light. There were his girls,
beaming. They looked at me and talked to him.
They were so happy he was home. They were so
happy that they could have breakfast in the dark.
They asked him why we smelled like smoke."

## 9.

"I got into his car. I asked him how he got hooked
up with this therapy group, and he told me he'd
decided to do it all on his own. He said he just drove

past the prison one day shortly after he and his wife ended their marriage and thought, You know, there are probably a lot of single guys in there feeling just like me. He told me he just went up to the front gate, asked to see the warden, and when the warden appeared asked if he thought anyone inside might be interested in getting together to talk informally about love and its absences.

"The warden laughed, apparently. My friend told me that the warden laughed and said that he doubted it, but that my friend could get a day pass and sit down in the field during a thirty-minute outdoor lunch to see if anyone came over. Then my friend said, 'And guess who now joins my little group of forty-five inmates every week?'

"'The warden,' I answered.

"'That fucker,' my friend said. He looked wistful. 'I love that fat fucker.'

"We were sitting in his car, staring at our houses. He'd stopped talking. I had nothing more to say. It was interesting to just sit and look at the houses, actually. I took a deep breath.

"'You like the new owners?' he asked me.

"'They're fine,' I said.

"'They'll disappoint you,' he said. 'That's the way it is with neighbors.'

"We had very little in common, generally speaking, aside from our property lines. We drove in silence and when we arrived I learned that the penitentiary parking lot is a vast—just absolutely sweeping—dirt desert that goes out beyond view for miles. From any particular spot in this desert, you have to walk about a quarter mile before getting to the prison's tiny entryway, which is shrouded by barbed-wire fencing. When they let you in, you pass through a maze of hallways of windowless cinder block, and you're patted down and scanned at every steel-barred gate, of which there are more than five between the entry and the open field where selected inmates can take a thirty-minute outdoor lunch. My friend and I went every step of the way through this in silence.

"Out on the lawn, many of the guys had already gathered, waiting for my friend. They were sitting folded-leg style in the grass. They eyed me as we approached. I sat down. My friend went to the front of them and stood. He lifted his hands and, when they'd quieted down completely, he thanked them for coming and for their willingness to *see the world beyond love*.

"The men were nodding. He continued. He spoke for some time on *the intrinsic colossal disaster of seeing love that isn't actually there*, and he used an example of two blind dogs he'd come to love when he was interning at a veterinarian clinic in North Carolina. The dogs had, apparently, died. He'd discovered them dead one morning. 'Just gone,' he said, his voice beginning to tremble. He snapped his fingers. He cleared his throat. He said he was devastated. He said he had never known devastation like this; no devastation since has ever compared, he said. He said he imagined we knew what he was talking about.

"The sun was exceptionally warm. I looked around again. One thing was clear from the expressions on faces of the men in that group: it wasn't a good idea to talk about dead dogs. They didn't like that. Some of the men began getting up. This agitated one of those still sitting. My friend kept talking as though the exchanges occurring among these men were trivial, subdued. Dead dogs, he said, were only a metaphor. But they were not. One man stood up, shoved another one from behind, called him a slur. The warden shifted and rolled up to his feet. I was trying to stand when three or four other men pushed me back down and jumped the warden, and the guy who hadn't, at first, gotten up to leave. They kicked him in the head. I saw the man's head moving in horrible angles. Three or four men kicking a head is a gruesome thing. Then the shots came and the yard was filled with weapons and shouting. I was on my stomach, pinned. I could see others pinned to the ground too."

## 10.

I look up at my wife. She's still sound asleep. We have a baby coming in the next few weeks, and she is sleeping so hard, for such short periods of time, in such odd physical contortions to fit her strange dimensions, I am amazed to see the way serenity can sometimes play across her face. We have been married six years. We have planned everything very carefully, very strategically, my anomalous heart attack and double bypass last year notwithstanding. We were ready, I had been thinking until this spate of divorces, to have this baby. I was uneasy that everyone was getting divorced. I tell her this. "It's crazy," I say. "What are divorces, anyway?"

## 11.

Eventually my friend turned on a few more of the house lights and seemed to loosen up. He told silly stories to his girls, and I drank a second beer. The television was turned on. His daughters described their favorite late-night television show to me. They said Jimmy Kimmel was *kank*, but he was also a little bit *smunt*. They could not have been six. My friend looked at me and shrugged.

Then I noticed my friend's wife had materialized in the kitchen, in a blue robe, holding a beer. She stood at the edge of the kitchen, just where the kitchen met the living room, and she asked what time we'd gotten home. My friend didn't answer, so I told her. I told her it was nice to see her again.

"Yeah," she said, as if she was asking me a question.

Then she asked about my wife. I asked her about her lawn. I complained about the housing market. She said she knew it was strange, but she loved crabgrass. We went on like this for a few minutes, talking small, my friend playing with his daughters by the television. She had come over to me and sat on the arm of my chair. She seemed entirely easy. She only looked in her husband's direction a few times.

"Well," I said. I stood up to leave.

She looked surprised. "Oh," she said. "You don't have to go anywhere."

"No," I said.

"Have another beer," she said.

She got up and went to the fridge, even as I was saying I shouldn't drink any more, and she opened that beer, twisted it with her bare hands, and brought it back to me. Then she went back to the fridge, opened another, and brought it to her husband. Then she told her husband, my friend, to sit on the sofa.

And he did. He got up from the floor and threw himself onto the sofa. She sat on his lap. "What else is new?" she asked me.

I hear you're getting divorced, I wanted to say.

"Very little," I said.

My wife is still sleeping as I tell her this. I tell her that when I looked up again, I saw the two of them—my friend and his wife—kissing on the sofa and I presumed, at first, it was a quick and conciliatory kind of thing. I looked at their girls, who were also looking at their parents.

They kept kissing. I looked again at the girls, and then back at their parents. The TV went to a commercial. I saw my friend's wife's tongue, and his hand slipped inside her robe. They were both still holding their beers. As soon as he dropped his beer on the carpet, I stood up. I patted the girls on their heads. They took this as a sort of signal. They didn't look at me. They turned and left the room with me, as if they were going to walk me to the door. Instead they went straight up the stairs to their bedrooms. I whispered "Good-night" to them, and they turned around.

### 12.

My cardiologist took particular care of me during my heart attack and subsequent surgery. He visited my room frequently. He said little, but he checked my stats with a sort of earnest determination, flipping papers, hammering things into his computer. The night before my surgery, after everyone had left, he came to my room and closed the door. He sat on the edge of my bed. He said, "You know what you need?"

"A hug?"

He looked at his watch. "I find most heart patients," he said, "need someone to scare the shit out of them."

"O.K.," I said.

"If you're not going to change your lifestyle . . ." he said. He looked at me. That's all he said. He produced a plastic model of the human heart from his coat pocket, and he stuck his fingers inside and started pulling it apart. He scattered the rubber pieces across my bedsheets and left.

## 13.

"C'mon," the older daughter said. She summoned me up. I followed. I went upstairs with them. At the top of the stairs, we turned to the right and went into a room lit only by candles. Inside, the walls were lined with mounted game. I stared at a zebra head. "Jesus," I said. The older daughter told me the zebra's name was Beverly. The fox was Lenny, the pheasant Jennifer. And the wild turkey had no name at all, because they had just killed it that morning.

## 14.

I take my head off my wife's lap and sit up. I upset the sofa cushions a bit, bounce a little, so that she'll wake up. I touch her shoulder. She wakes up. She smiles. She wipes her face. She reaches into a stretch, and she brings her hands to her stomach, to our bursting child inside there. She tells me she feels like hell, and I say I know what she means. She rolls her eyes. "Take me upstairs," she says. I consider this. I consider carrying her. I consider her weight. "C'mon," she says. I put my arm under her legs. I support her back. I lift her. Her eyes close. Her mouth sags. It's chilly. The gravel path is lit only by dull moonlight. There's a breeze. The crickets are calling. I hear the waves lapping at the shore. I hear my boat rubbing the wooden pier. The rope moorings are aching. The cabin is dark. I put my wife down on our creaking bed. I stand upright and look at her form. It's no easy journey getting her here. I wish we lived closer.

# SCANDAMERICAN PASTORAL

"**D**on't you fucking tease me," she says. But I'm not teasing. I have manufactured an afternoon alone, the two of us. I am thirsty, very dry. "But why?" she pleads. "How?"

I can't remember the answer to these questions. It all seems so complicated in retrospect. It might've been just one phone call. We deliver the children by their armpits to her sister.

We're off like fugitives. We drive and spar. Then silence.

The mall strikes me as larger from the outside, smaller and more angular on the inside. I feel my hands needing occupation. I look around my feet, the tile flooring, certain I've dropped something. I pat my pockets. She demands I tell her what time it is. I am rocking from one foot to the other.

We search for things that have been needed at some point in time, but I can't determine if the listed price of an ottoman is reasonable, or if it's suddenly through the roof, the way it feels to me, sort of, I really can't remember, and she can't remember the space the ottoman was supposed to fill—do we even need an ottoman? Is it an ottoman, or was it a fish tank?

In the fish tank, fish—small carp—spawn. It's a vicious visual experience. She's gone instead for French lip balm, returns with nothing. She needs *advice*!

We lunch. Strange breadless pizza—robust, god-awful huge—is smoking in front of us.

She demands the time.

I am bored. She is tired. She naps on a leather sofa, beside an elderly man who has allowed her to place her head on the cushion next to him. The man covers her with newspapers to keep her warm, and I fix my gaze on the way in which well-waxed tile floor refracts the soles of rubber shoes an instant before the sole.

I get up to buy wrapping paper in a cheerful store. The magnetic stripe on the credit card doesn't work.

I rouse my wife. It is time to collect the children again. The sun blazes at an odd angle. It is fall. We have started a new season. There is a light that almost fills the car.

# LAST COTTAGE

We know the Larsons. They come to Slocum Lake each summer. We would like them to stop, but they do not stop. For fifteen years, they have come to Slocum Lake to stay at their place on the waterfront. They own the only remaining cottage on the lake; they possess the only waterfront property that has not been commercially developed. Here, in Slocum Lake, we could use that development. We desperately wish they would sell. Instead, they bring their children and teach them the ways of traditional summertime Slocum Lake living. It's very depressing, it's very outmoded, and our tolerance is pressed.

In June, someone paid to have someone electrocute Slocum Lake, to stun and then kill some of the fish. It wasn't terribly expensive. A collection was taken. The more expensive part of the process involved gathering the dead fish and corralling them into the part of the lake that runs about twenty yards out from the Larsons' beachfront, and approximately fifty yards across. The expensive part, actually, was installing the concealed netted cage that kept the dead fish where we wanted them—mysteriously pent up against the Larsons' beach.

The Larsons always arrive on one of the first days of July. They roll in at nighttime. We presume they are sheepish people. It is possible their drive down from the north of Wisconsin is longer than we know it to be, because perhaps their children make them stop frequently. We don't exactly know. We know they arrive late at night, as a general annual rule. We know they carry their children into the cottage, put them in their respective bunk beds, knock off the bedroom lights, lock up, and walk down to the beachfront.

This year, they arrived this way again. When they walked down to the beachfront, they held hands. Their hot truck engine was still ticking in their gravel drive. Locusts were scorching the ears of the trees on their property, the only native trees remaining on the waterfront, inglorious poplars. Summer had come very early to Slocum Lake. The locusts had hatched early too. The nights were very warm and still. The Larsons exchanged a few inaudible remarks. Their shoulders were rubbing.

Once they reached the waterfront, they turned to face one another, held one another, and kissed. They kissed for quite some time. They have kissed before, in years previous; they usually stop kissing and go into the water together. This year, they did not go into the water. They dropped onto their knees and continued kissing. Then Robert Larson took his shirt off, and we thought this signaled a move they might make toward the water. We were wrong. Robert embraced his wife very hard. Then he slipped his wife's shirt over her head.

They were kissing with great force, it seemed, and it seemed they would not stop kissing. Then they stopped kissing. We thought this was it. Instead of rising from his knees, however, Robert lowered himself onto his back. His wife, Penny Larson, laughed and put herself on top of him. It was dark, and we believe they then made love in this position. We watched it, thinking they would go swimming after, but instead they only made docile, unremarkable love, gathered their clothes, and ran naked back toward their cottage. They were laughing, but when they stepped onto the porch, they stopped laughing and were very quiet as they slipped in through their screen door. They never turned on any house lights. They simply vanished into the dark of their little, dwarfish cottage that everyone on Slocum Lake wanted to blow up.

We would not want to hurt the Larsons. The Larsons are good people with good intentions. They leave their home in northernmost Wisconsin and head south, just as everyone in Illinois not affiliated with Slocum Lake and its general and perpetual state of impoverishment goes north to summer on the largely virgin beachwater up there. No doubt, the Larsons know exactly what it feels like to have strange people perching on your property, behaving as though it were their own just because they purchased it from you. We actually feel for the Larsons as people.

We feel for them enough, in any case, that we try not to be awkward about our determination to oust them. We believe confronting them would be awkward and, in the end, because it would likely change nothing, needless. Instead, we have for years determined to be chilly and unwelcoming. We believed this would be enough. Then they had the children, and we could see the future we imagined—fiscal and otherwise—being denied us.

Two years ago, facing this reality, someone who did not identify himself vandalized the Larsons' boat launch. Last year, we decided as a community to vandalize their roof. We tore large holes in their shingles with hammers late at night, in February. We believed the water damage from spring runoff would give them pause. They came in early July, studied the damage, left to stay at a hotel, and simply had someone come and rebuild the roof and interior. It was Bernie Benson they hired to do it, and he couldn't be bribed into doing shoddy work, as no one outside of Chicago can be bribed in this way. Their roof is now better than any roof of ours and their interior looks like a catalog image.

The Larsons could not be heard at their windows, so we retired; we returned just after dawn. The children were awake. They are darling children, twins, towheaded beauties. They ate breakfast in their pajamas, careful not to wake their parents. They poked each other without laughing, covering their mouths with their hands, and spoke about their dreams for their vacation. They are good children, and we decided on the dead fish because it would impact them directly. We knew the Larsons would not like their children impacted. We believed we could impact the children without devastating them.

The sun had risen over the buildings on the eastern shore, and it was already blasting the buildings on the western shore. The insects had moved from the water to the grass, because the water was warmer than the air temperature. The insects were horrific, biting savages. You never get used to that. Time waiting in such conditions is not terribly pleasant. You look at your watch a lot.

Even with their central air conditioning, installed the year of the children's arrival, the twins had become a little restless. They had already dressed for swimming—at the age of four years, these remarkable, delightful twins, had dressed all by themselves. Then they slipped out of the cottage, careful not to let the screen door slam. They ran to the boat, which was still hitched to the Larsons' car. They pulled back the protective covering and climbed inside the boat, under the covering. Every year, they play inside the boat. We do not know what they do in there. We presume they play make-believe games. We think it is peculiar that children from so far north play with boats the way that children from down here do. We often think that, for children and adults from the north, boats are just like old wallpaper.

They were laughing and giggling in the boat for the better part of an hour. Eventually, they slid out from under the covering, hopped off the boat, and returned to the cottage. They were inflating their toys just as their parents emerged from their bedroom and sat down beside them on the renovated floor. The Larsons kissed their children on their heads and their hands and petted their hair, and you could see the sort of bliss in the eyes of the Larsons we desired very determinedly to remove.

Shortly thereafter, the children at last received approval to go down to the beachfront, and Robert and Penny stood up to watch their children run from the porch of their cottage down to their sandy beach. The children ran as quickly as four-year-olds can run, shoeless and in minimal swimming-wear. Both were topless; the girl's bottoms were nearly obscene, and the boy wore only a baggy pair of briefs. We recognize that the Larsons felt they were alone on their property; we believe, had they realized the public dimension of their daily events, they likely would have dressed their children differently. Certainly they would have exercised greater restraint in letting their children run down to the beach and plunge, half-nude, into the infested water. We know the Larsons well enough to grasp they are not reckless, thoughtless types. Like many people from Wisconsin, actually, they are prudent and wry. They remind us of our grandparents.

The Larson children tumbled face-first into the water. For approximately two minutes, they rolled and played in innocence. They laughed and splashed and spread themselves lengthwise in the water. Then the boy screamed. Then the girl screamed. The two of them burst into a series of unpleasant sounds.

The Larsons sprinted from the cottage. They were pained. Their robes were encumbrances. The situation was tense, mortal. We had never seen Robert Larson move so swiftly. He shed his robe as he neared the water; Penny Larson's leg gave out, just at that moment, and she slipped, bent awkwardly, slid several feet, then lifted herself, clutching her knee, and continued running, hopping toward the children. Robert by then had hoisted them from the water. Penny took the girl. Penny and Robert exchanged only a few words in agitation, but we heard what we needed Robert to say: "The beach is covered in dead fish."

Indeed. We waited. They walked quickly to the cottage, the twins in their arms. They went inside. There was very little to be heard. We believed we could see Robert pacing, if briefly, before emerging again and walking down to the water, where he kicked the fish with his sandaled foot. He covered his mouth and nose with his hand. The fish smelled even worse once you realized what you were smelling. Robert then shielded his eyes with his other hand and surveyed the water. From that vantage, dead fish carcasses spread out for what must have seemed miles. We'd paid good money for this.

There had been a fair bit of talk about the way to kill the fish. Plenty of the lake's sportsmen felt the need for careful electronic culling, separating the game fish—bass, bluegill, catfish—from those fish whose role in the lake seemed, by sportsmen standards, unclear. The mayor's office and Parks and Recreation, who in the end were footing the largest portion of the bill, contended that such careful culling would require an exorbitant amount of additional cash, and that it was cheaper to restock the game fish than to cull and restore them once the electrocution was completed. Poets and local liberal activists like myself argued that the impact would be lessened if we merely blitzed the Larsons and their children with dead fish of all types. Rather, we argued, if the fish were carefully selected—bottom-dwellers, suckers, waterway leeches—there would be no mistaking the message we were trying to send. It would be difficult, in other words, for the Larsons not to recognize a careful plan at work and to see themselves symbolized as sucking fish, disgusting bottom-dwellers left for dead on their beach.

Robert Larson moved slowly back up the sand, his hands in his pockets. He entered the cottage.

He looked at his wife and shrugged. Then Penny shrugged. Then Robert Larson shrugged again. Then he said, "Nature down here is funky," and he clicked his tongue and sat down.

The children, these fine and very sweet and well-mannered twins, were glancing back and forth between their parents, very forlorn and very anxious. Larson looked at his wife, and Penny looked at him. Larson nodded. The children darted through the screen door and ran to the beachfront again. They plunged into the water and seized the fish in large quantities, held them against their bodies, and threw them at one another. They lobbed them in various ways—like footballs, like hand grenades. They kissed them and pretended to fall in love with them, then they threw them back into the water, jilted. They rode on top of the big ones like dolphins. They pitched them onto the beach; some of the carp were more than five feet long, and by working together, the children were able to drag them onto the sand. The twins then began making forts and castles with them. We held our mouths.

We might have kept holding our mouths had Larson not sped out of the driveway. We turned to see him go. He drove quickly, but the stop signs slowed him. He had his arm out the window. He spat tobacco onto the road. He had his music on loudly—a local radio channel, country western, not from the Chicago towers but from those in Kankakee. He turned into the Cat rental facility on the north end of Route 176, went inside, and according to Davis, the manager, rented a small skid steer loader for one half day at a holiday rate of 175 dollars. Davis also covered the cost of delivery, which would take place later that afternoon, as there was no demand for skid steers at that time. Repelling open or clandestine bribes is one thing; facilitating the enemy is really something entirely different. We sometimes look at Davis and wonder what Slocum Lake would feel like without him.

Larson stopped off at the Island Foods grocery. He called his wife two times on his cellular phone while he stood, looking uneasy, in the meats and seafood department. He bypassed the local bakery doughnuts and took three boxed Danish rings, the national brand. He brought his items to the counter and had the clerk fill several paper bags. He used coupons. He slid his credit card. He pushed his cart to the truck, dropped the bags in the back, and returned the cart to the rack by the store entry. We never doubted his goodness. He drove back to the cottage and joined his wife, who was sitting on the porch watching the twins bury each other in fish carcasses.

That night, the Larsons barbecued the carp on an open grill and somehow managed to swallow it. Penny served the fillets with a mayonnaise and dill relish. We had not seen Robert purchase the dill. After dinner, the kids climbed into their bunk beds, and the Larsons went down to the beach and rearranged the carp the kids had strewn across the sand. Given our distance, we did not know they had organized the fish into a sort of soft bed until, as they had the night before, they lay down to make sustained love.

Words cannot bring clarity to the feelings we had while watching the Larsons make love on top of the carp. *We felt very depressed* might be about as close as we can get. We left the Larsons' cottage to have meals with our own families. We figured we were back to the drawing board. We figured we had not impacted the children in the right way, and had failed to alter the Larsons' iron grip on their ownership of Lake Slocum waterfront property. Because of our depression, we had not foreseen Robert Larson's critical error.

Thankfully, we were not so depressed that we didn't return the next morning, just after dawn. The twins were again playing in the boat, and Robert was already awake, running the skid steer, scooping large quantities of the carp and shunting them from the waterfront to the back of his property, where he had—apparently before sunrise—dug a massive grave for the fish. It did not strike all of us at the same time, but the image of Larson hoisting the fish and steering them away from our water gave one of us, and then every one of us, a rather brutal jolt.

We called Princess at the Parks and Recreation office to confirm the limit of carp a person could take from Slocum Lake on any single fishing day. Princess told us what we all well knew from the bylaws of the constitutional charter on fish repara-tion: one hundred carp is the maximum any one licensed person can catch and keep on a given day. We asked nicely if Princess would send someone over to have a look at the load of carp Mr. Robert Larson had taken from our Slocum Lake.

The fine for violating the charter ran one thousand dollars alone; the fine for each violating fish ran one hundred dollars per fish; the fine for not having a license issued by the state of Illinois for taking any fish from the water, one hundred dollars. Princess herself came over with a clutch of Slocum Lake police officers to hand the Larsons their ticket for two hundred fifty thousand dollars. She explained that the police estimated Larson had extracted no fewer than twenty-five hundred carp from Slocum Lake, and she pointed down into the massive pit. It would be difficult to doubt that estimate, certainly. She continued explaining that Parks and Recreation was actually, probably, estimating low, and they were willing, also, to give the Larsons a break on the other violations and round off at a quarter of a million dollars, due October first of the current fiscal year.

She touched Robert's shoulder and said, "We only take money orders for fines that exceed one hundred thousand, Mister Larson, but we know we can trust your personal checks around here." Princess winked.

Robert Larson winced and recoiled from her hand. He attempted to explain that the fish were already dead, but Princess waved him down—

irrelevant and subjective. Robert protested a second time. Princess simply extended the ticket. Robert refused to take it. Princess placed it on the ground near his feet. Robert raised his voice. The children came out from the boat to watch. The police officers adjusted their belts and crossed their arms. Princess withdrew. Robert picked up the ticket. He was sweating so completely, the sunlight glinted wildly off his face.

Robert took the ticket to the porch, where he had a brief conversation with Penny. They shook their heads. They retreated inside. Their children—so bright and sensitive—grasped the gravity of the situation and went inside, settled down into Indian-style sitting and played cards with one another for the duration of the afternoon. The Larsons held protracted, at times heated, dialogues inside the cottage. The skid steer simply sat out in the sun. Some of the carp baked in their pit, and still more lapped against the shoreline.

The sun shifted its weight against the east-facing side of the shore. Evening came and went. Night tumbled in. We were pretty drunk by then. Someone had brought tequila. We had a great deal to celebrate. We took a shot every time Robert Larson rubbed his eyes. We breathed very easily when the house went dark. We assumed we would retire early to our families. But then we heard the Larsons slip out of their screen door and head down to the beach again. Rabbits! They took each other's clothes off and made love in the sand. They experimented a little bit. The locusts were screaming. The insects were loathsome. The Larsons rolled about for forty minutes, then ran naked back into their cottage. We wondered if we had all seen this, or if the most drunk of us had imagined it. How strange, these Larsons. What was Slocum Lake property to the kind of people who could make love in the face of its certain loss?

How brazen. We'd had someone at our bank evaluate the Larsons' portfolio: There was no way they could afford the fines. We shook our heads. These people from the northern fringe of Wisconsin were very much like our grandparents in so many ways. We knew them, and yet we knew them not at all.

We drank to this. Then we had a few more drinks. We became increasingly easy with one another as the night wore on. We did not return to our homes and families. We kissed a little bit ourselves, touching each other's limbs in the night. We became stupid in lust and mouthed one another. We did not hear Robert Larson leave the cottage. We did not at first hear the skid steer ignition. Sensuality creates a noise that cannot be rapidly punctured, but in time it became clear we were not hearing the thrumming of our bodies but rather Robert and the skid steer shifting gears in the middle of the night.

We cleared our throats and straightened. We had to adjust our eyes. We tapped our watches. Robert Larson was scooping out the grave of dead fish and, it became clear, trundling his scoops down to the beach, where he was dumping them into his Shamrock 270 diesel. He had launched the Shamrock in the afternoon. It was a detail that meant very little to us while we were drinking. He was working very quickly with the skid steer. No sooner had he dumped a load into the Shamrock than he was racing back up toward the cottage, behind it, to the grave, to collect another scoop. Then, back down to the beach and the boat. We tried to divine the meaning of this activity.

We discovered Penny Larson had also left the cottage and gone down to the water. She was in over her waist. She was wearing only a bra. She appeared to be moving the fish closer to the sand. She did not speak. She did not luxuriate. She seemed entirely devoted to the fish, a sort of shepherd, and we were perplexed until Robert emptied the grave and turned his scoop to the shoreline. Then the Larsons' intentions were made horribly clear and vivid to us. As Robert Larson loaded carp into the Shamrock— hoisting all our work and money very high in the air, water pouring from the hinges in the metal scoop, and dumping them with heavy thuds inside of the gunwales—we could see, very plainly, that Robert Larson planned to scuttle his fiscal and moral obligations to Slocum Lake. We were just sick. If the insects were draining us at that point, we were entirely unaware. We held each other.

And in what was surely less than thirty minutes, while we looked on, Robert Larson had filled his boat with every last fish from the grave and our mostly invisible netted cage. The sun was just beginning to illuminate Slocum Lake. The Larsons' boat sat low against the mooring. Robert killed the skid steer engine and hopped out. He walked the dock and stepped into the boat. With Penny's help, he proceeded to cover the top of the boat with its seasonal covering, snapping the canvas top over the entire keel, covering the fish with a sort of tightly fitted pall.

That's when one of us lost it. It was unspeakably hot. Heat like that, even under less demanding circumstances, is cruel. Half of us were naked or drunk. All of us were slick with sweat. It's not surprising that one of us would break from our cover and rush the Larsons' cottage with a burning poplar branch in his arms.

Perhaps he thought the rest of us would join him. Perhaps the heat had harmed him. Perhaps he could just no longer operate in clandestine rage, as we all were, and let the Larsons prolong our suffering and embarrassment another year. But there he was—the Kubicka kid, we believed—thrusting a burning, limpid poplar branch at the Larsons' kitchen window, yelling the word *crimes* over and over again at the top of his childish pitch. Try as he might, he could not in the end break through the window with this flaming branch. The limb bent and splayed each time he thrust. But the boy kept at it, jabbing, stepping back a few steps and charging, jousting, shouting *crimes!* It was painful to watch, and we did what we could: We called him away. We tried to flag him down. We implored him to drop the branch and return to us. But Robert Larson ran quickly to apprehend the Kubicka boy. Had Larson been faster, he might have stopped the fire from torching the wooden shingles of the cottage. In that heat, the siding and the roof went up like gasoline. Penny had followed Robert and slipped inside the cottage. She emerged with their beautiful children, groggy, and pointed them down to the beachfront, away from the cottage.

The Larson kids, so precious, walked down toward the dock in silence and did not raise their eyes. Had the cottage not caught fire, the children would probably never have gone down to the water. But it did, and they did, and we owe a great debt to the Kubicka kid, whom we have never seen since. Robert Larson grappled with the lithe Kubicka boy in the grass beside the burning cottage until the boy broke from Robert's grip and fled into the dark glow of dawn.

Robert did not follow. He grabbed the hose, turned on the house spigot, and began dousing the fire before it could race to the other side of the cottage. Penny took down a pickax from the porch. She yanked the burned and burning siding away from the house and spread it across the lawn. She whacked at the flames when they flared up. To watch these two was like watching junior amateur firefighters in earnest judged competition, a sort of marvel of meticulous and urgent care, and all the while their children, those wonderful blond twins, stood in pajamas by the dock, watching the smoke rise from the last cottage on our Slocum Lake.

Those beautiful children, dear god, to think of them. So good. What we loved most were their good natures. They never knew mistrust. They never asked questions or doubted strangers. You could tell them to go inside the boat, lie down among the carp, that their mother had instructed you to help them bed down inside the boat, beneath the cover of the boat, and to close their eyes. And they would not doubt you. They would not fuss. They would not fear.

You could sing them a quiet song, hum a melody, and you could touch their fine hair, brush it from their cheeks, over their ears, and they would curl to the feel of your knuckles, and they would smile as their sleep took them back. You don't always know what you're doing in this sort of Slocum Lake midsummer heat, but the Larson kids could just slip beneath the canopy of a boat and never say a word, even as you snapped the cover securely over their heads. Those tender kids, the last thing you'd ever see of them, their hands folded beneath their chins; that image could just shake you to the core, shatter your soul in a million ways.

And then we receded, and we watched Robert descend to the beach and the dock, and there we held our breath. Penny was scrambling around the inside of the house, working the interior wood paneling and insulation for any trace of smoldering. Robert Larson unmoored the boat, unlashed the tethers from its side, and hopped into the water. From there he pushed on the stern and, straining, moved the heavy, low-riding boat into deeper water. He pushed and built momentum until Slocum Lake was over his neck and nearly in his mouth. Then he let the boat go. In the placid water, it skated silently over our nearly invisible netted cage and into open water. No breeze touched its gentle, steady wake. Out it went.

Robert pulled himself on the dock and watched it go. Then he bent down, dripping, and lifted a rifle to his shoulder. He closed his eye. He aimed and, from his knee, fired two quick, resonant shots. We turned. We saw the boat pitch. It lurched, dropped, then plunged into the depths of Slocum Lake with enormous emissions of escaping air, like the blowing of cattle gas.

Then silence. Just like that. The hot Slocum Lake water was still. Our carp were gone, returned to the gunk of our lake bottom, and with them all our efforts to fleece and harry the Larsons. We felt some remorse. We do not like to devastate children, after all. But the sun was coming up. It shone on the Larsons' cottage. We waited. We watched Robert Larson walk inside, shower, and then sit down on their cottage's fine wood floors beside his wife. They talked as the sun rose. Penny had poured coffee. They wiped their eyes and their foreheads. They studied the fire damage to their interior wall. It was minor. They smiled and shook their heads. Then, as if pricked, Penny stuck up her head. We could see in her eyes the sudden flaming of awareness. She opened her mouth and ran to the empty bunk beds. She returned to Robert. She trembled. She took his shoulder. They began calling out the children's names. They searched the cottage. They moved outside to search the property. They yelled out. They shouted. They screamed in ways we could not have predicted. They ran to the water. They shielded their eyes from the sun in searching. Robert waded in several steps, and then he turned around to look at Penny. His face, we could see, was rent. He yelled to the skies above us all for states around. He entered and left our chests. We know the Larsons, yes. We have known them for years. Now we know they know loss. Now we know they know us.

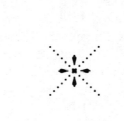

# ACKNOWLEDGMENTS

Several of these stories first appeared in the following publications: "Of Pigs and Children" (*New Delta Review*), "Check the Baby" (*Gulf Coast*), "In Lapland" (*Gettysburg Review*), "Local Accident" (*New World Writing*), "Scandamerican Domestic" (*Smokelong Quarterly*), "Direct Assault from South Sweden" (*New World Writing*), "Time in Norrmalmstorg" (*Laurel Review*), "When Our Son, 26, Brings Us His First Girlfriend" (*New South*), "O Sweet One in the Bluff" (*New World Writing*), "The Cook at Swedish Castle" (*Black Warrior Review*), "Tomtens" (*Fairy Tale Review*), "When Our Son, 36, Asks Us for What He Calls a Small Loan" (the *Collagist*), "Cabins" (*SubTropics*), "Scandamerican Pastoral" (*Gulf Coast*), and "Last Cottage" (*Cincinnati Review, Best American Mystery Stories 2011*).

I want to thank the editors of the literary journals that took a chance on my work. In particular, I want to thank the editors who really went out of their way to work with me on some of these stories in various stages: Frederick Barthelme, Matt Bell, Sean Bishop, Chris Chambers, Brock Clarke, Andrew Farkas, Michael Griffith, Tara Masih, Meg Pokrass, and Richard Sonnenmoser.

I am a living product of American academic creative writing programs, and I have therefore enjoyed the privilege of learning from and working with many really wonderful teachers. Thank you Padgett Powell, Nancy Reisman, David Leavitt, Brian Kiteley, Selah Saterstrom, and Laird Hunt. My first teacher of fiction is also the one I need to thank the most thoroughly, because he has stayed with me year after year after year: Josh Russell, a prodigious friend, stunning writer, and staggeringly smart teacher.

The good people at Coffee House, who also took a risk on me. The first books I fell in love with were Coffee House Press books, and your invitation into this press is really a dream for which I am so grateful.

I want to thank my devoted and generous parents, my awesome sister, and my nutty and lovable extended family in Illinois.

And finally, of course, there's only one person in my life who has been with me from the first story in this book to the last: Molly, thank you. You are the smartest, sharpest, kindest, cutest, wisest person I know, and I am lucky I get to share a name and house and kids and bedsheets with you.

# FUNDER ACKNOWLEDGMENTS

Coffee House Press is an independent, nonprofit literary publisher. Our books are made possible through the generous support of grants and gifts from many foundations, corporate giving programs, state and federal support, and through donations from individuals who believe in the transformational power of literature. Coffee House Press receives major operating support from Amazon, the Bush Foundation, the Jerome Foundation, the McKnight Foundation, from Target, and in part from a grant provided by the Minnesota State Arts Board through an appropriation by the Minnesota State Legislature from the State's general fund and its arts and cultural heritage fund with money from the vote of the people of Minnesota on November 4, 2008, and a grant from the Wells Fargo Foundation of Minnesota. Support for this title was received from the National Endowment for the Arts, a federal agency. Coffee House also receives support from: several anonymous donors; Suzanne Allen; Elmer L. and Eleanor J. Andersen Foundation; Around Town Agency; Patricia Beithon; Bill Berkson; the Patrick and Aimee Butler Family Foundation; the Buuck Family Foundation; Claire Casey; Jane Dalrymple-Hollo; Ruth Dayton; Dorsey & Whitney, LLP; Mary Ebert and Paul Stembler; Chris Fischbach and Katie Dublinski; Fredrikson & Byron, P.A.; Katie Freeman; Sally French; Jeffrey Hom; Carl and Heidi Horsch; Alex and Ada Katz; Stephen and Isabel Keating; Kenneth Kahn; the Kenneth Koch Literary Estate; Kathy and Dean Koutsky; the Lenfestey Family

Foundation; Sarah Lutman; Carol and Aaron Mack; Mary McDermid; Sjur Midness and Briar Andresen; the Nash Foundation; Peter and Jennifer Nelson; Rebecca Rand; the Rehael Fund of the Minneapolis Foundation; Schwegman, Lundberg & Woessner, P.A.; Kiki Smith; Jeffrey Sugerman and Sarah Schultz; Nan Swid; Patricia Tilton; the Archie D. & Bertha H. Walker Foundation; Stu Wilson and Mel Barker; the Woessner Freeman Family Foundation; Margaret and Angus Wurtele; and many other generous individual donors.

To you and our many readers across the country, we send our thanks for your continuing support.

## COFFEE HOUSE PRESS

The mission of Coffee House Press is to publish exciting, vital, and enduring authors of our time; to delight and inspire readers; to contribute to the cultural life of our community; and to enrich our literary heritage. By building on the best traditions of publishing and the book arts, we produce books that celebrate imagination, innovation in the craft of writing, and the many authentic voices of the American experience.

To join our community of readers, please visit coffeehousepress.org.

# RECOMMENDED BY
# CHRISTOPHER MERKNER

### Horse, Flower, Bird
Stories by Kate Bernheimer
ISBN: 978-1-56689-247-6
"Each of these spare and elegant tales rings like a bell in your head. Memorable, original, and not much like anything else you've read."
—KAREN JOY FOWLER

### I Hotel
A novel by Karen Tei Yamashita
ISBN: 978-156689-239-1
"*I Hotel* is an explosive site, a profound metaphor and jazzy, epic novel rolled into one. Karen Tei Yamashita chronicles the colliding arts and social movements in the Bay Area of the wayward '70s with fierce intelligence, humor and empathy."
—JESSICA HAGEDORN

### The Cosmopolitan
Poetry by Donna Stonecipher
ISBN: 978-1-56689-221-6
"Donna Stonecipher's mesmerizing *The Cosmopolitan* is a travelogue of consciousness, a diary of displacement whose writing self seems simultaneously nowhere and everywhere ('And isn't nowhere, after all, also an elsewhere?')."
—JOHN KOETHE

### Windeye
Stories by Brian Evenson
ISBN: 978-1-56689-298-8
"Brian Evenson is one of the treasures of American story writing, a true successor both to the generation of Coover, Barthelme, Hawkes and Co., but also to Edgar Allan Poe."
—JONATHAN LETHEM

**COLOPHON**

*The Rise & Fall of the Scandamerican Domestic*
was designed at Coffee House Press,
in the historic Grain Belt Brewery's
Bottling House near downtown Minneapolis.
The text is set in New Caledonia.